PIG REMO

Chiun had intercepted the note meant for Remo. It said: "Pig Remo, I wait for you in the intended place. N."

Out in the hot, deserted oil field, Chiun, Master of Sinanju, faced Nuihc, who aspired to be Master.

"You should pray to your ancestors for forgiveness," Chiun said softly. "You go now to meet them in another world."

Nuihc smiled thinly. "Have you forgotten that you may not kill another from the village?"

Chiun answered, "No, I will not kill you. But I will leave you here in broken pieces and let the sun finish the task I am not permitted to complete."

And then Chiun took a step forward. And another. And another.

Niuhc backed away. Chiun was in front of him. Nuihc turned. He felt a whir as a yellow hand flashed over his head. He gasped and bolted to the right. But there . . . again . . . Chiun stood before him, a spectre of death and destruction in black. And there was nowhere else to turn.

THE DESTROYER SERIES:

#1	CREATED, THE DESTROYER	#23	CHILD'S PLAY
#2	DEATH CHECK	#24	KING'S CURSE
#3	CHINESE PUZZLE	#25	SWEET DREAMS
#4	MAFIA FIX	#26	IN ENEMY HANDS
#5	DR. QUAKE	#27	THE LAST TEMPLE
#6	DEATH THERAPY	#28	SHIP OF DEATH
#7	UNION BUST	#29	THE FINAL DEATH
#8	SUMMIT CHASE	#30	MUGGER BLOOD
#9	MURDER'S SHIELD	#31	THE HEAD MEN
#10	TERROR SQUAD	#32	KILLER CHROMOSOMES
#11	KILL OR CURE	#33	VOODOO DIE
#12	SLAVE SAFARI	#34	CHAINED REACTION
#13	ACID ROCK	#35	LAST CALL
#14	JUDGMENT DAY	#36	POWER PLAY
#15	MURDER WARD	#37	BOTTOM LINE
#16	OIL SLICK	#38	BAY CITY BLAST
#17	LAST WAR DANCE	#39	MISSING LINK
#18	FUNNY MONEY	#40	DANGEROUS GAMES
#19	HOLY TERROR	#41	FIRING LINE
#20	ASSASSIN'S PLAY-OFF	#42	TIMBER LINE
#21	DEADLY SEEDS	#43	MIDNIGHT MAN
#22	BRAIN DRAIN		

ATTENTION: SCHOOLS AND CORPORATIONS

PINNACLE Books are available at quantity discounts with bulk purchases for educational, business or special promotional use. For further details, please write to: SPECIAL SALES MANAGER, Pinnacle Books, Inc. 1430 Broadway, New York, NY 10018.

WRITE FOR OUR FREE CATALOG

If there is a Pinnacle Book you want—and you cannot find it locally—it is available from us simply by sending the title and price plus 75¢ to cover mailing and handling costs to:
Pinnacle Books, Inc.
Reader Service Department
1430 Broadway
New York, NY 10018
Please allow 6 weeks for delivery.

—— Check here if you want to receive our catalog regularly.

THE DESTROYER: OIL SLICK

by
Richard Sapir and Warren Murphy

PINNACLE BOOKS • NEW YORK

THE DESTROYER: OIL SLICK

Copyright © 1974 by Richard Sapir and Warren Murphy

All rights reserved, including the right to reproduce
this book or portions thereof in any form.

An original Pinnacle Books edition, published for the
first time anywhere.

ISBN: 0-523-41231-2

First printing, August 1974
Second printing, November 1974
Third printing, March 1978
Fourth printing, August 1978
Fifth printing, March 1981

Printed in the United States of America

PINNACLE BOOKS, INC.
1430 Broadway
New York, New York 10018

For the most unique Charley I know, and for the glorious House of Sinanju, P.O. Box 1149, Pittsfield, Massachusetts.

CHAPTER ONE

"No greater enemy exists than one's own illusion of safety."—House of Sinanju.

He was a big one. Standing upright, he could reach the topmost branches and in one bite consume the terrified man-apes hiding there. A swat of his giant paw could crack the sabertooth's spine like a dried twig.

But nothing was dry here in the lush foliage, where each step oozed into muck and the very air steamed from the rich, tropical growth as Tyrannosaurus Rex thundered through the swamp.

In drier climates, others of his species would leave their bones for the descendants of the man-apes to piece together for their museums. But this would be thousands upon thousands upon thousands of years later, when the man-apes ruled the earth.

For now, the man-ape was only a tender morsel, scrambling desperately through the treetops, where branches touched and mingled.

Since Tyrannosaurus feared no enemy, he moved along without looking down, his eyes searching the branches for any man-apes too slow to have fled. Then a hind leg went into the muck just a little too deeply.

The danger signal flashed in the tiny, bird-sized brain. With his other hind leg, the giant animal tried to lift himself, but that leg sank even deeper.

As the creature sank, the small front paws grasped at a tree, but only tore it muck-sucking from its flooded roots. With a raging bellow, the Tyrannosaurus swallowed slime and then settled into the soft ooze.

One terrified man-ape, hidden in the treetop high above, watched as the huge hulk sank out of sight beneath him. His primitive brain wondered only briefly if there was any way he could get a piece of that massive meat, now sliding away from him. He soon forgot the thought.

No matter, the man-ape was alive for a while longer and what he did not know and could not perceive was that his own descendants, who would walk easily on two legs and who would not need the trees for protection, would need the Tyrannosaurus's body for survival more than he did. His descendants would fight and scheme and lie over the monster's body.

For even as the oxygen stopped coursing through the giant reptilian body, a strange chemical change was beginning. The body was beginning to rot, and along with smaller bodies and foliage it would decompose under great pressure, and over many thousands of years, these decomposed carbon-based bodies would form a black liquid called oil.

The black liquid moved under the earth as if alive. It passed easily through porous stones or openings, until it hit a cap of unporous rock that prevented it from moving upward. When water pressure from below prevented it from moving back downward, it became a stable, motionless, very accessible pocket of oil. All a man would have to do would be to sink a hole through the capstone and out would gush dark, black crude.

When that happened, the Tyrannosaurus's body would

be indistinguishable from any other organisms, even the occasional body of the ape that would become man. They would all be crude oil, and because of a difference of merely pennies a barrel for their liquid remains, the industrialized world would almost manipulate itself into bankruptcy.

The ground above the particular pool of oil to which this Tyrannosaurus had contributed its remains gradually changed from swamp to jungle to sandy hot desert. The area became a Phoenician trading post, then a Roman city, then trackless desert again. Finally it was resurrected by Italians, whose presence and wealth attracted roaming Berber tribesmen.

In the Arab nationalism of the late twentieth century—according to Western measures of time—the land above the Tyrannosaurus's body became known as the Revolutionary People's Free Arab Republic. To most of the world it was still known as Lobynia, a name it had carried for centuries, until the deposing a few years before of its king, His Islamic Majesty Adras.

While new history books reported that the king had been deposed by the heroic struggles of the illustrious Arab people's revolutionary fervor, the great page in Arab heroism had been helped along by Seagram's Seven Whiskey.

The king's personal pilot, Pat Callahan of Jersey City, N.J., U.S.A., had been drunk the week of the revolution, and only the Lobynian Air Force's chief of staff, Muhammed Ali Hassan, was available to fly the king's jet from the Swiss health spa he had been visiting back to the Italian-named capital of Dapoli.

When King Adras heard that revolutionary forces were taking over the palaces and the Royal Lobynian Radio Station, he offered Callahan five thousand dollars in gold to put down his bottle of Seagram's Seven, sober up immediately, and fly him and his German bodyguards back to Lobynia.

"Oh, Majesty, I would be honored to fly you for nothing," said General Ali Hassan, chief of staff of the Lobynian Air Force.

"Ten thousand dollars," said King Adras to Callahan, who was trying to get to his knees.

"How much is that in rials?" asked Callahan, who had been working for the king for five years now. But before King Adras could answer, Callahan passed out in the hotel suite.

"I will fly you through storm and flak and over ocean and under clouds. I shall carry your royal majesty in grandeur like the eagle. I go where you command," said Air Chief of Staff Ali Hassan.

"Try going away from me," said the king, who had $250 million worth of Mirage jets rusting on Lobynian airfields, an investment made to show royal confidence in the Lobynian Air Force, whose leading pilot was none other than its commander, General Ali Hassan.

Hassan was so good, said his fellow Muslims, that he could almost fly a jet without a Frenchman as copilot. When Ali Hassan had made his first solo in a Piper Cub, Lobynia promptly bought the jets. They never touched a cloud again.

Thus, when his Air Force chief of staff was the only one capable of returning him—or, more accurately, *willing* to return him—to Lobynia, King Adras decided to reassert his royal presence by making a long-distance telephone call.

With the help of the Swiss national police, he finally got a call through to his palace.

A young colonel answered the phone.

"Where is my minister of defense?" asked the king.

"In jail," said the colonel.

"Where is the commander of my armies?"

"Fled to Morocco."

"Who are you?"

"Colonel Muammar Baraka."

"I don't remember you. Describe yourself."

"I scored highest on the entrance exam in the history of the royal military academy."

"I don't place you."

"I lead the Lobynian armor on your birthday parade."

"Oh, yes. The Italian-looking fellow."

"Correct."

"Well, you are now a general. I have just promoted you. Crush the rebellion. Shoot the traitors and clean the blood out of the palace before Friday." King Adras looked at the unconscious Callahan, still clutching his bottle of Seagram's Seven. "Make that Saturday," he said.

"I am afraid I can't do that, your majesty."

"Why not?"

"I am the leader of the rebellion."

"Oh. I guess you're ready to face my German bodyguards?"

"They have no way of getting here and besides every man, woman, and child has lifted his voice in the revolution. We will tear you and your imperialist reactionary lackey to shreds. We will burn your eyes out, tear your limbs. Today we have taken the first step towards Arab glory and civilization."

"This doesn't mean a complete stop to my income, does it?"

"Not necessarily. A king who does not try to regain his crown can live very comfortably."

"May Allah bless the revolution."

"May Allah bless his majesty."

"Use the Swiss banks. They're more experienced in

these matters. And don't worry about the legend of my family crown."

"What legend?" asked the colonel.

"It is said that when my family ruled Baghdad ... I am not a Berber, as you know."

"That helped considerably with the revolution."

"When we had the caliphate of Baghdad ... this was way before that sergeant declared himself shah ... well, in any case, it is said that when an ambassador from an eastern country wished to present the most magnificent gift he could think of, he gave my ancestor—the caliph—a promise. This promise, he said, was worth more than gold, more than rubies, more than the finest silks from Cathay."

"Get to the point."

"*I'm* telling the story," said King Adras.

"I don't have all day."

"Well, to make a beautiful, long story short and ugly, what he gave was the promise of the services of the finest assassins in the world. He who takes the crown from the head of any of the descendants of the great caliph will reap a whirlwind from the east. But it will come from the west."

"Anything else?"

"No."

"Long live the revolution. Good-bye." And the young colonel hung up the phone and did not think about the fanciful tale, one more tool of reactionary forces, until he held the industrialized world by a ring through its nose. And the ring was what the Tyrannosaurus's body had become. Oil.

And at first, just like the Tyrannosaurus, Colonel Muammar Baraka was afraid of nothing.

CHAPTER TWO

His name was Remo and he was ready.

He did not have to be told he was ready, because if he had had to be told, then he would not have been ready. He could not feel he was ready because the knowledge was beyond feeling. It was a knowing so quiet, so beyond far and yet so close at the same time, that when it was there one knew it.

It came to him, not during nerve-chilling exercises and not during his balance tests as he hovered twenty stories above the street on a narrow hotel ledge. It came to him in his sleep in a hotel room in Denver, Colorado. He opened his eyes and said:

"Wow. I'm ready."

He went into the bathroom and turned on the light. He looked at himself in the full-length mirror behind the door. It was more than a decade now since he had started, and if anything, he had lost ten or fifteen pounds since then. Thinner. Definitely thinner. But he still had the thick wrists. They had been nature's gift; everything else he had been taught.

He dressed. Black socks, tan slip-on shoes of Italian leather, gray slacks, and blue shirt. He had dark eyes and high cheekbones, the flesh drawn taut under them. There hadn't been any more operations to change his face recently, and in the last few years he had learned, if need be, to change it himself. It wasn't that hard, and anyone could do it. It was just a matter of tiny changes, muscle manipulations within the mouth, a tensing of the scalp around the hairline, a change in the cast of the eyes. When most people tried it, they looked as though they were making a funny face, because they forgot and did one thing at a time instead of making all the changes simultaneously.

The hotel hallway was silent when he slipped out, and Remo Williams did not bother to lock his room. What would anyone take, anyhow? Underwear? Slacks? So what? And if they should take money, so what again? What could he spend it on? He'd never be able to buy a home, at least not one to live in. A car? He could buy all the cars he wanted. So what?

Money was not a problem. He was told at the beginning that he would never have a money problem again. What they didn't tell him was that it wouldn't make any difference. It was as though someone were assured that he would be free from attack by flying saucers. Well now, isn't that nice?

No, there was different treasure now, that no one could take away from him. Remo stopped in front of the adjacent hallway door. Well, only one person could take it away. That one person was sleeping in the adjacent room. His teacher, Chiun, the Master of Sinanju.

Remo took an elevator down to the lobby, hushed in its deep night wait until morning would make it alive with people again.

When he and Chiun had checked into the hotel the day before, Remo had looked out the window and said, "There are the mountains."

Chiun had nodded almost imperceptibly. The frail wisp

of a beard on the yellowed parchment face seemed to shiver.

"Here it will be where you must find the mountain," he said.

"What?" Remo had said, turning to Chiun, who was sitting on one of his fourteen gaudily lacquered steamer trunks. Remo wore all his clothes. When they became soiled, he threw them away and bought new ones. Chiun never threw possessions away, but he chided Remo for his white American materialism.

"It will be here," said Chiun, "and you must find the mountain."

"What mountain?"

"How can I tell you, if you do not know?" asked Chiun.

"Hey, don't play philosopher with me, Little Father. The House of Sinanju is a house of killers, and you're supposed to be an assassin, not a philosopher," said Remo.

"When something is so good, some one thing is so glorious, then it must be many things. Sinanju is many things and what makes us different from all those that have ever been before is what we think and how we think."

"God forbid Upstairs should miss one payment to your village, Little Father; they'll find out how philosophical you are."

Chiun thought a long moment while he looked at Remo. "This may be the last time I look at you the way you are," he said.

"Which way? As what?"

"As an inadequate piece of a pale pig's ear," said Chiun with a high cackle before he disappeared into a separate room. He did not answer when Remo knocked. Not for morning exercises nor for evening advancement did the Master of Sinanju respond to Remo's knocks, even though during the day, Remo could hear the dull television voices of the soap operas in which the Master of Sinanju found pleasure. Thus it was for several days, until Remo was awake and aware that he was ready.

It was cool that spring night in the mile-high city, and while Remo could not see the great Rockies ahead of him, he knew snow was there. At a street corner, he stopped. The snow would melt and whatever destruction the winter had done to life would be exposed. If not buried in some dry place, elk or man or fieldmouse would rot in the sun and become part of the soil and of the mountain which had been there long before life tiptoed over its crust, and which would be there long after life was buried in it.

Ten years ago, when Remo had started his training, he did not think of such things.

He had been framed for a murder he had not committed. He had thought he was being executed but had awakened to find he had been selected as the enforcement arm of a secret organization that did not exist.

It did not exist because public knowledge of it would be an admission that the United States Constitution did not work. Its job was secretly to balance the books that had tilted on the side of crime. Remo, as its assassin, was the chief bookkeeper. "Violate the constitution to save the constitution," the young president who created the secret organization named CURE had said.

Only three men knew what it was and what it did. One of them was the president, another was the head of CURE—a Dr. Harold W. Smith, director of the Folcroft Sanitarium research center in Rye, N.Y., that served as CURE's cover—and Remo.

After he had been recruited from the electric chair, Remo had been put in the hands of Chiun, an aged Korean, for training in the assassin's art. But not even Dr. Harold W. Smith of Folcroft could have anticipated the changes that the training would make. No computer could have projected what the human body could do, not even if they had fed in data calculated on the per gram strength of an ant times the balance of a cat.

They had selected one man and his body to be a tool to serve a cause, and ten years later he found himself using the cause to serve the tool.

Remo felt the mountains and knew this. He was who he was, and he realized now he had always known this. It was the mountain that Chiun had told him he must find, the mountain of his own identity.

Over the decade the Master of Sinanju had shown through training, through pain, through fear, through despair, just what Remo could be, and now that he understood it, he knew that what he could be, of course, was just what he had always been.

Done. Then he knew. So this was it. As Chiun had said, the truth is a common thing. Only fairy tales glitter like rubies in a crystal universe.

"Hey, gringo. What you looking at, eh, gringo?"

The voice came from behind a parked car. There were eight of them, none taller than Remo. Cigarette butts gleamed in the black, moonless night. Down the street a traffic light became green and nothing moved.

"Hey, gringo, I talking to you. You Chicano or gringo?"

"I was thinking and you interrupted me."

"Hey, Chico, he thinking. The gringo is thinking. Everybody shut up, the big gringo, he thinking. What you thinking, gringo?"

"I'm thinking how lucky I am to be upwind from you."

"Hey, the gringo, he smart. The gringo he real smart. Heavy, man. Gringo, no one tell you this is Chicano territory? This is a Chicano street. I Caesar Ramirez. You need my okay to go thinking on my street, gringo."

Remo turned and walked back toward the hotel. He heard one of the youths yell something else. Then they were following him. When one got so close Remo could feel the hot breath on his neck, Remo caught him by the lips and yanked forward, pulling the arching body over in front of him, before walking into the young man's descending spinal column. Pop, crack, that was it; the body was a lifeless bag of flesh. When the sanitation men found it the next day, the hips and shoulders would not be connected by bone.

Immediately knives were thrust at Remo's back. In a little dance step, without changing direction or stopping, Remo continued moving toward the hotel.

One knife wielder came close and Remo took his wrist and fenced off another knife. He did this in a very simple way. He popped blade into brain and suddenly the second blade no longer faced his stomach.

Remo kept walking toward the hotel, still carrying the first knife wielder's wrist. Then one more came at him and made the mistake of getting between Remo and his hotel. It was Caesar and he saw Remo's face and decided to get out of Remo's way, but he changed his mind a moment too late.

While the city of Denver would pay for Caesar's funeral as it had paid for his birth, his house, his food, and his schooling (where he had learned to call all this sustenance oppression, though he did not feel oppressed enough to get a job), somehow the city of Denver had deserted him now in his moment of need. Caesar found himself within arm's length of the crazy gringo. Alone. Without even a social worker to help. And that was all.

No more Caesar.

Chico, whose wrist had been borrowed for the fight, bawled and demanded it back. Without looking, Remo casually tossed it over his shoulder. It landed at the young man's knees.

Back at the hotel, he knocked on the door that had not answered for the last few days.

"Little Father," he called. "I have found the mountain. I always was what I am now. The ignorance has been removed."

And now there was an answer.

"Good. Then we are ready and we will be found." Chiun had been saying the same thing for weeks and Remo had not understood it. But now he did. He knew what Chiun meant by saying that they would be found, and he knew by whom.

"I understand, Little Father," he called.

And from another nearby room came an angry growl.

"Hey, you out there, shut up or I'll come out and close your mouth for good." And since Remo had nothing more to say, he went back to his own room and back to sleep, realizing that a mountain was a thing you climbed or fell from, but not a place where you rested.

CHAPTER THREE

The first thing Dr. Ravelstein noticed about the badges was that they were upside down. If the two men in the neat gray suits were really from the FBI, wouldn't their badges be right side up in their billfolds? Then again, Dr. Ravelstein had once met an FBI man while getting a security clearance, and didn't he use an identification card instead of a badge? Oh well, no matter.

"I can't make out your badges," said Dr. Ravelstein. He was tired. It was 3:30 A.M. and since 9:00 A.M., the day before, he had been looking at greenish printouts from the terminal connected to one of the University of Michigan computers. With his tired fifty-year-old eyes, he probably couldn't have made out whether the agents had shown him badges or sliced salami, he thought. Thinking about his tired eyes, Dr. Marvin Ravelstein, professor of engineering, suddenly realized that his eyeglasses were not in front of his eyes. He had put them somewhere when he had heard the door in the laboratory open.

"If you put on your glasses, you might make out our identification a little better," said the larger agent.

"Yes. The glasses. Where are they?"

"On your head."

"Oh, yes. Yes, of course. Who are you? Ah, yes, Special Agent Paul Mobley and Special Agent Martin Philbin. I see. Yes. Very good. Very good. Very good. Well, thank you for dropping by. It's been nice having you."

"Sir, we've come to discuss something very important. You may be the man who can save the world."

Dr. Ravelstein sighed and nodded, indicating stools near his laboratory bench. Outside, the unseasonable spring heat made the Michigan campus a muggy sock of a night. In here, his own cigarettes combined with the air conditioning to turn the air into a bitter environment, especially if it had to be endured for more than six hours at a stretch. Dr. Ravelstein nodded to himself again. What the FBI men had said was correct. He not only *could* save industrialized society from bankruptcy, he had done it. And the amusing part was that the numbers had told him he was a success, not the tangible products in the other room. Those could be touched by anyone and anyone could say this is fine crude oil over here and this is a marvelous new building material over there, but not until the computer digested massive marketing facts, did he know that he was successful. His months-old suspicions had been borne out just twenty-five minutes ago. Twenty-five minutes, and it had taken the government bureaucrats no longer than that to get their sticky fingers into the pie.

"Can save the world?" said Ravelstein. "I have, if you must know. At least, I've given it a twenty-year reprieve. I suppose I'm in for some sort of a prize if that means anything at all. Actually, gentlemen, I'd rather have a good night's sleep. What can I do for you? Please make it brief. I'm very tired."

"We have reason to believe, Dr. Ravelstein, that your life is in danger."

"Nonsense. Who would want to harm me?"

"The same people who killed Dr. Johnson of Rensellaer Polytechnic Institute."

"Erik is dead? No," said Ravelstein, sinking softly into his chair. "No. I don't believe it. I don't believe it."

"Late yesterday. His back was broken in a fall. It looked like an accident, but it wasn't. It was as accidental as a sniper shot. One of his assistants saw the two men push him down an elevator shaft," said Special Agent Mobley, the larger one.

"Yeah, it was said that he put up a real struggle for a man his age," said Philbin, his thin, pinched face apparently mournful.

Was the agent laughing at him from behind that mournful face? Did that agent think there was something funny about Dr. Johnson's death? No. Impossible. It must be the hour. It was so very late.

"I'd like to call the Johnson family."

"At this hour, Dr. Ravelstein? Perhaps they have just gotten Mrs. Johnson under sedation. You don't know, do you?"

"Are you sure he was ... he was killed?"

"Yes. He made a tragic mistake. His work in hydrocarbons came too close to providing a substitute for gasoline," said Mobley.

"Oh, he had that for years," said Ravelstein. He lit a cigarette and offered the two men the pack. They refused but Mobley lighted the cigarette for Ravelstein, who sucked hungrily on the smoke. At this hour, he didn't even enjoy cigarettes any more. Then again, he thought, how many cigarettes a day did he ever enjoy? One? Possibly none.

"What do you mean, he had that for years?" asked Agent Mobley.

"Erik had the gasoline substitute for years. Don't you gentlemen understand what the oil crisis is all about? The whole energy crisis has got nothing to do with the amount of energy or whether we can find more. There is more energy available than man can ever use. He'll be trampling himself to death for lack of space before he runs out of energy."

Dr. Ravelstein watched the shock on the faces of the two agents. It was always like that. As if one of the major problems of industrialized society was as mysterious as an eclipse to a savage.

"You mean the Johnson gas substitute was not a solution?" asked Agent Mobley, his beefy face squinted in disbelief. "He died for nothing?"

"Died for nothing. Died for something. Dead is dead. I don't know why people consider some sorts of death noble."

"You were saying, Doctor, about Johnson's substitute being no solution."

Ravelstein smiled. He lifted up the heavy folded computer printout forms and handed them to Mobley.

"Here. This is the solution."

"It's a chemical formula?" asked Mobley.

Ravelstein laughed. "It is not. It is a collection of freight charges, building needs, labor costs, the rising prices of cement, brick and stressed concrete. Estimates, of course, but America now has an estimated twenty-year solution to its energy crisis. It's a reprieve."

"I don't understand. Where did you find a substitute for oil?"

"I didn't. I found a substitute for brick, cement, and aluminum. I found a substitute for asphalt. I found a substitute for wood."

Philbin looked at Mobley as if they had stumbled into a sleep-crazed loony. Mobley ignored the silent communication. He felt his palms become sweaty holding the printout. He knew he was hearing the truth.

Dr. Ravelstein lifted a small blackboard from his desk.

"Don't hold that printout as though it's diamonds. It's

only a map. A way out of the energy crisis. Are you following my train of thought?"

Mobley glanced suspiciously at the printout. "I think so," he said hesitantly.

"No, you aren't," said Ravelstein. "All right. It wasn't until 1970 that the United States began depending on oil imports. Not because we didn't have oil, but because it was cheaper to import oil from the Arabian gulf than to pump it at home. It becomes more expensive with any well as you get near the bottom. I don't know if you knew that."

"I didn't know that," said Mobley.

"We could be sitting on a pool of oil right now and be out of oil—economically out of oil, that is—just because it is too expensive to pump out of the ground. We have literally oceans of oil in shale. Oceans of it."

"But it's too expensive, right?" said Mobley.

"Was too expensive," said Ravelstein.

"Well, even I know you have to process tons and tons of shale to get oil. Tons and tons," said Mobley.

Dr. Ravelstein grinned mischievously. "That's right," he said. "Tons and tons of worthless shale to get out the oil. The oil would be priced skyhigh. Too high to be of any use to the driver, to the corporation, to the utilities. No one could afford it. That was what was wrong with Dr. Johnson's gasoline substitute. It cost three dollars a gallon to produce. The country can't run on three-dollar-a-gallon gas."

"So what's your solution?" asked Mobley.

"Come. I'll show you."

"C'mon, Philbin," said Mobley. Philbin nodded dully and hitched up his shoulder strap. Dr. Ravelstein saw the handle of a .45 caliber automatic and thought it was strange because he had been under the impression FBI men used only revolvers because revolvers were said to be less prone to jamming. Or was it that they used only automatics? No matter, it was not his field.

He led the two men to a small door; it opened without a key.

"If whatever you've discovered is in there, shouldn't you have it under lock and key?"

"I guess working with criminals so much you've developed a criminal mind," said Ravelstein. "What's in there is free, anyhow. As free as commonsense." He opened the door and turned on the lights.

"I guess I shouldn't have bothered turning off the lights. We're all going to have as much cheap energy as we can use for the next twenty years. Gentlemen, here it is."

"Here what is?" asked Mobley as he heard Philbin chuckle. All he saw was a pile of bricks, some thin wallboard, and a bin of dust.

"Gentlemen, here is brick, here is wallboard, and here is cement. They're all economically competitive, and they're all made from shale."

"I think I get the idea now," said Mobley. "That printout back there had nothing to do with oil needs, did it?"

"You'd make an excellent student, Mr. Mobley. What do you think those figures were about?"

"They were about bullshit," said Philbin. He tapped Mobley on the back. "C'mon, let's do what we gotta do instead of hanging around here pulling on our ears."

Mobley gave the thin man an icy look.

"I think," he told Ravelstein, "those printouts were about America's building needs for the next decade."

"Not only America's," said Ravelstein. "South America and Asia, too."

"You mean there are transportation figures in there, too?"

"Right," said Ravelstein. "Now for an A plus, tell me the cost of producing oil by my method?"

Philbin looked bored. Mobley looked astonished. "Not a penny," he said. "Brilliant. You produce salable building material and what's left over is the oil. The key is not taking the oil out of the shale, but making use of the shale with the oil left over. Fantastic. Where do you keep the formula?"

"In my head," said Dr. Ravelstein. "But it's no great discovery. A simple process which most chemical engineers could duplicate if asked to do so."

"Thank you," said Philbin and unsnapped his shoulder holster. Dr. Ravelstein watched in fascination beyond horror. He saw the smaller man take out a large gun that somehow fit very well into the small hand. He saw the flash around the barrel and nothing else. His last thought was, "I do not believe this is happening to me."

He experienced no terror nor even a wish that what he saw transpiring should not transpire. He made a very accurate and dispassionate assessment of the situation. He was going to be killed. And then he was.

Paul Mobley watched the elderly head snap back with a big fat red hole in the center of the skull. Ravelstein hit the laboratory floor like a sack of his own shale cement.

"You damned idiot. What the hell did you do that for?" Mobley yelled at Philbin.

"That's what we're supposed to do instead of standing around here jerking around."

"We were supposed to close down Ravelstein's research. Burn his formulas. Steal his samples or whatever we found. We were supposed to stop his project, not necessarily kill him."

"A little blood bother you, Paulie?" laughed Philbin, putting his gun back in its holster. "C'mon, let's get out of here."

"Out of here, you idiot?" Mobley's beefy face flushed red. "What good will it do to get out of here?"

"Take that printout and let's go."

"Weren't you listening? The printout isn't the key. It's these building materials. Somebody takes a good look at these and Ravelstein might as well be alive."

"But they don't have the formula to make the stuff, Paulie. Come on, let's go."

"They don't need the formula, idiot. Didn't you hear him? Any chemical engineer could do it, if he was told to."

Lights went on across the campus. They heard footsteps running up the stairs. The weary elevator motor hummed into life.

"Come on, Paulie, come on," said Philbin desperately.

"We can't go without this stuff."

"I'm going, Paulie. I don't want to wait for the cops."

"We either face the cops or you know who."

"He don't have to know."

"You think he ain't going to know?" asked Mobley.

"Oh, Jesus," whined Philbin.

"Shut up and listen this time." Mobley outlined a plan.

When the campus watchmen barged into the laboratory, Mobley flashed his badge and immediately demanded to know who the watchmen were. His tone was harsh and authoritative, with a lingering ring of suspicion.

They were old men, these campus guards, retired machine operators or gas station attendants, whose main job was filling a blue uniform with an official-looking badge that had no more legal power than a belt buckle.

Mobley had no trouble badgering the watchmen into servitude. Had any of them ever attended a murder scene in an official capacity before, he would have realized one did not wrap the victim in a canvas bag or just trundle out large objects as evidence.

21

"This box is heavy," said one of the watchmen, grunting behind a large crate of pinkish powder.

"Yeah," said Philbin. "We need the fingerprints."

"What do we have to bring the whole thing for?"

"Because I say so," said Mobley. The watchman was used to such explanations and he didn't ask any more questions. Also, he couldn't have cared less, which seemed to be the prevalent attitude of campus watchmen everywhere.

When the body and the cement and the wallboard and the bricks were loaded on the campus maintenance trucks, the night watchmen were informed that their presence would be required at FBI headquarters.

To a man, the university employees had one question.

"Do we get overtime?"

"Absolutely," said Mobley. "The FBI guarantees it. You've got a federal guarantee."

That the FBI could not authorize someone else's payment of funds did not occur to the watchmen who had helped load what they thought was evidence. They had a promise from someone in a white shirt and tie who had an official-looking badge and the magic word was "overtime."

So they drove off that predawn spring morning in the small truck, and that was the last time they were seen on the campus of the University of Michigan in Ann Arbor.

They were driven to an abandoned football field where they were told to mix water with the pinkish powder and when the crate of strange cement became gooey, they were all given an eternity at time and a half from the barrels of two .45 automatics.

"Kill one or four, they only hang you once," said Mobley.

"They don't hang you ever, these days," laughed Philbin.

22

"Yah. The law doesn't. Unfortunately, you-know-who does."

" 'Deed I do," said Philbin. " 'Deed I do."

And they left the football field in the cab of the small truck, which they soon parked on the bottom of a river. Dr. Ravelstein, three watchmen, cement, wallboard, and bricks went down with their truck.

Dr. Ravelstein's disappearance was noticed the next day.

The disappearance of the three night watchmen was only discovered by the University a month later, when an administrator finally noticed that three employees had not been showing up for work.

Because of this incident a symposium on university-employee relations was held. The chairman of the communications department presided. All groups were invited to participate to "achieve maximum meaningful participation." The conclusion of the symposium, called "Outspeak," was that there was a lack of communication between employees and the university. The only reasonable solution was to double the budget of the communications department in "a massive stopgap restructuring of employee relations through radical communications techniques."

Then Dr. Ravelstein's body floated up from his own cement, along with the three campus guards. The funny pink substance clinging to their bodies was analyzed and found to be a component of shale.

In what appeared to be a sanitarium in Rye, New York, on the shores of Long Island Sound, information on Dr. Ravelstein's death, along with the death of Dr. Erik Johnson, found its way into the same file. This was done by the computer, which also noted that the substance on Ravelstein's body was shale without oil.

These facts hit the desk of the director of Folcroft, and he found a pattern in them.

The pattern was energy. And death for those who found new sources of it.

CHAPTER FOUR

"What do you know about oil and energy?"

Remo Williams heard the question while focusing on his left pinky knuckle. He was seeing if he could make it jump. Not that there was any purpose in making one's pinky knuckle jump. But it was either that or concentrate on what Dr. Harold Smith was telling him, and that was almost as annoying as looking at Dr. Smith who had picked the only straight-backed chair in the room and started talking nearly a half hour before about this scientist floating up in some river and that scientist going down some stairwell.

Remo's feet were propped up. Above his left pinky knuckle, through the hotel window, were the Rockies. Next door, Chiun was watching the last of "The Rampant and the Beautiful." This month, half a dozen of the main characters were getting abortions—the viewer knew this because the best friends in the story were telling everyone else. They were supposed to be friends, because they looked very sad when they disclosed these things under the pretext of sharing problems. In real life, this would be called vicious gossip. In "The Rampant and the Beautiful," it was called helping.

Remo heard the organ music of the daytime drama

through the hotel wall. He heard Smith's sharp New England whip of a voice pick at him. He decided he loved his pinky knuckle.

"What do you know about oil and energy?" Smith repeated.

"Everything there is to know. Everything that will be known, and everything that was once known but is now forgotten," said Remo, who started a race between his thumb knuckle and pinky knuckle, the loser to be unloved for the rest of the afternoon.

"You're joshing, of course."

"Would I fool the man who framed me for murder, then sent me out to kill?"

"This seems to be a recurring problem on your part," Smith said. "I thought by now that you understood it is necessary that you be officially dead to insure that there is no record of you anywhere. The man who doesn't exist for the organization that doesn't exist. It has to be that way."

"Yeah, I guess," said Remo, allowing the index finger to join the contest.

"Are you looking at your knuckles or listening to me?"

"I can do both, you know."

"What are you doing with your knuckles, anyway? I've never seen anyone do that. That's amazing."

"All you have to do is devote your life to it and you can master it, too, Smitty."

"Hmmm. Well, I suppose you have to occupy yourself some way. Seriously now, what do you know about oil and energy?"

"Everything."

"All right. What's a hydrocarbon?"

"None of your business."

"Well, that settles that. Let's start at the beginning and this time look at me."

So for another hour, Remo looked at the lemon-faced Smith while he detailed the problems of oil, both economically and criminally, and explained why he had decided that CURE must get involved, even though the situation was technically outside the organization's jurisdiction. If the country came apart, he explained, it would make little difference whether the constitution existed or not.

"And energy is more dangerous in its aspects than atomic weapons, Remo."

"That's terrible," said Remo, looking at Dr. Smith's pale blue eyes, while exercising the balance of his arms in continuity by the ever-so-slight touching of his fingernails. Every few minutes, Remo repeated, "terrible, awful, horrible," until Smith said:

"What's horrible, Remo?"

"Whatever you said, Smitty. This oil thing."

"Remo, I knew you were barely listening. Why do you continue in service? I don't think you care about America anymore. You used to."

"I do care, Smitty," said Remo, and now he was looking at that crusty New England face, with the majestic snow-crowned Rockies rising behind it, out past Denver. Behind Remo were the American plains and the big old cities. Behind Remo was where America had fought a civil war, losing more men than in any other war. Behind Remo was where bloody strikes and bloody company goons wrote labor history.

He had been born back there in the East, and abandoned, which was why he could become a man who didn't exist. Who would he feel required to contact again? Who would miss him?

Folcroft Sanitarium was back there, and that was the second time Remo was born, and this time he knew more about life.

"I continue to serve, Smitty, because that is what is right. The only freedom anyone has is to do right."

"The moral thing, you mean."

"No. Not necessarily. Those mountains behind you are the most mountain they can be. They are, and they are right. I must be that, too. It came to me while I was here. I am what I am. And what I am is ready."

"Remo. For a wise-guy Newark cop, you're beginning to talk like Chiun. I don't think I have to remind you that Sinanju is a house of paid assassins, centuries old. We pay Chiun's village for his services. We paid for your training."

"Smitty, you're not going to understand this, but you paid for what you wanted Chiun to do, not for what Chiun did. You wanted him to teach me parlor tricks of self-defense. He taught me Sinanju."

"That is absurd," Smith said. "You're talking nonsense."

Remo shook his head. "You can't buy something you don't understand, Smitty. You'll never understand . . . Now why not get on with the assignment?"

Smith smiled wanly and proceeded to outline the problem and the assignment.

Problem: the Arab nations were putting a slow oil squeeze on the United States. American researchers working on oil substitutes had been killed.

Assignment: a physicist at Berkeley is working on another oil substitute; see that he isn't killed. Secondly, find out who is behind the killings.

Smith explained it carefully. When Remo appeared to be secure in his knowledge of priorities—nowadays it was often more important whom he didn't kill—Smith thanked him, zipped his flat, worn briefcase, and headed for the door without offering to shake hands.

At the door, Chiun appeared, vowed the eternal loyalty

of the House of Sinanju to the beneficent Emperor Smith, shut the door behind CURE's director, and said to Remo:

"One does not give an emperor too much time. He begins to think he knows how one does things."

"I like Smitty. For all my problems with him, I like him. He is one of my people."

Chiun nodded slowly, and like a gentle blossom on a soft cushion of warm air, descended into a sitting position from which to speak. The golden kimono settled around him.

"I have not told you this, but even though Koreans are my people, not all are wise and brave and honest, nor do all serve their discipline with integrity."

"No crap," said Remo, feigning surprise. "You mean to tell me that all Koreans aren't wonderful? I can't believe it."

"It is true," said Chiun and solemnly repeated a story Remo had only heard two hundred times. When the supreme power made man, he first put the dough in the oven and took it out too quickly. It was underdone and no good. That was the white man. He put more dough in the oven and to make up for his mistake in making a white man, he left the dough in too long and made the black man. Another mistake. But after the first two failures, he got it just right and out came the yellow man.

And into this man he put thoughts. And the first thoughts were disproportionate to the human mind, breeding arrogance. And that was the Japanese. And into the next man he put thoughts that were inadequate and stupid. And that was the Chinese. Since thoughts are very complicated, the supreme being kept trying and failing, and he created the piggy Thais, the corrupt Vietnamese, the . . .

Chiun frowned a moment. "Never mind the details. The rest were pig droppings. But when the supreme being made Koreans, he got it just right. The right color and the right mind. But what you have just discovered through my

And Chiun began listing the faults of all the provinces and villages until he came to one and that was Sinanju, his tale was that not even all Koreans are perfect."

ancestral home. But before he could finish, Remo did something he had never done before.

"Little Father. Because of what Sinanju produced, both you and I may someday be killed. I know that you brought me here to make me ready to face that challenge, and now I am ready. But remember, that challenge comes from Sinanju. Not only from Sinanju, but from your house. From your very family. The better became the worse and both of us are still looking over our shoulders because of the evil that came out of Sinanju."

And with that, Remo turned and left the room in high discourtesy to the latest Master of Sinanju.

Riding down in the elevator, he thought of the evil from Sinanju, which was Chiun's nephew, Nuihc. Nuihc had been the son of Chiun's brother. He would have succeeded Chiun as the Master of Sinanju, but he had turned to crime.

Twice before, he had tried to kill Remo and Chiun. Twice, he and Remo had battled to standoffs. The second time, Chiun had warned Remo: "When we want him, he will find us." It would, Remo understood, be their greatest challenge.

And he knew that this was the reason Chiun had brought him here. To make sure he was ready for that challenge, which Chiun, in his unerring way, knew would come soon.

Remo was ready; he knew what he was now, and what he had always been. But he allowed himself to wish that Nuihc had been drowned at birth in the North Korean sea.

Remo caught a cab to the airport, found out the schedule, saw the delays, and went right outside and hailed another cab.

"Downtown," he said.

"Where downtown?" the driver asked.

"You got the sentence wrong, buddy. Not where downtown, but downtown where."

"Okay," said the weary driver. "Downtown where?"

"Berkeley."

"You're kidding," said the driver. Remo pushed three one-hundred-dollar bills through the change chute at him, which killed all the driver's objections but one. He wanted to go home first, to get a change of clothes and tell his wife where he was going.

"I'll pay for a change of clothes. You're making the drive nonstop anyhow."

"But I've got to tell my wife where I'm going, you know."

Remo threw two tens into the front seat, but the driver explained that he and his wife were very close. They were very close up to fifty dollars, when she became nosy and possessive. Remo slept all the way to Berkeley. He arrived at the science building just in time to see the fourth floor of a large red brick and aluminum building come blasting across campus. Shards of glass sprayed a half-mile into downtown Berkeley, cutting only 227 undergraduates who had been manning booths to collect signatures for the legalization of marijuana. Ugly billowing black smoke belched from where the fourth floor had been. People started running toward the building. The nervous blare of a siren sounded far away.

A dark-haired coed in tee shirt and faded jeans covered her face, weeping.

"Oh, no. Oh, no. Oh, no."

Remo rolled down the cab window.

"That's the science building, isn't it?" he asked.

"What?" she sobbed.

"Science building, right?"

"Yes, it's awful. How could anything like this happen?"

Remo rolled up the window.

"You should have made it faster through the Rockies."

"I got you here late, huh?" said the driver.

"Yes and no."

"I just hope there weren't people in there," said the driver. He had the look of horror that comes when people realize that life is not as secure as they have themselves convinced. The look would disappear as the driver once again rebuilt the illusion that he was not in fact at the gates of death with every breath he took.

"That's awful," he said. "To think it could happen here."

"Where should it happen?"

"Well, somewhere else."

"Like death. Death happens somewhere else, right?" said Remo.

"Well, yeah. Yeah," said the driver. "It should happen somewhere else." He stared as ambulances were loaded at the building, some rushing away with sirens on high, others taking a slow, even pace. They were the ones carrying the dead.

"Whoever did that ought to be punished," the driver said.

"I think you're right. Sloppy work should always be punished."

"What do you mean?"

"I mean, dear driver to whom I am trying to give a greater tip than just money because he is an American of my own blood, there is one sure thing that will be punished in this world and that is doing something wrong—making a wrong decision or making a wrong move. That's

32

always punished. Evil? Well, maybe that's just an extension of wrong thought."

"What the hell are you talking about?" asked the driver, shaking behind the wheel. Firemen were lowering bodies from the charred holes in the fourth-floor wall. The driver was not looking at Remo, but at the bodies.

What Remo was talking about was that the person who had blown up the science building had committed suicide just as surely as if he had put a gun to his own temple. He had made a mistake; he would be punished. But Remo was tired of talking and got out of the cab.

The Denver cab driver badly wanted to get back across the Rockies. He presumed that in Denver university buildings did not go up in roaring blasts.

Remo watched him speed away. But the driver was so shaken and confused that he picked up a fare at the corner, who got out just as quickly as he entered. As he backed out the fare stared at the driver as though he were insane. The cab drove off; the fare remained, standing on the corner and scratching his head, watching the out-of-state plates move away.

Remo strolled onto the Berkeley campus, annoyed that the college scientist who had been working on a way to harness the sun's energy was probably dead, and that somebody had been crude enough to use a bomb to try to destroy an idea.

"It's awful, it's awful," sobbed a woman in white laboratory coat. Her blonde hair had frazzled black ends, not the roots but the ends that had obviously felt the fire of the explosion. She was talking to a young reporter behind a fire engine that sat useless before the entrance to the science building.

The reporter, a young man who looked as if he had slept in his gray suit, then rolled through lunch with it, was taking notes.

"The FBI warned us about a possible attempt on the doctor's life, but we thought it was just fascist propaganda."

"What did they say?" asked the reporter.

"They said there might be an attempt on the doctor's life and . . . oh, god . . . they examined the lab for bombs but there weren't any and then they left and then, oh, god, it was awful . . . the wall came in. The whole wall. Like it was dust. And then there was the fire and then I couldn't hear anything."

"You there," said Remo sternly. "Who told you you could speak to reporters?"

"I didn't . . ." said the woman, but she couldn't finish her sentence.

"Not until we get everything cleared up first. Then you can talk to reporters."

"Who are you?" asked the reporter.

"Strategic Security," whispered Remo in hushed tones of confidence. "That doctor's death may not mean beans. We already have everything we need. All they killed was another human being. I'll talk to you later. This is off the record."

And the reporter, having heard a government official say that a human life was unimportant, contentedly moved on to interview other people, secure in the knowledge that he had a contact who would not only hang himself later, but probably take his own department into complete embarrassment with him. He did not even bother to ask what Strategic Security was.

Remo found out from the woman with the frazzled hair that the two FBI men had carried a briefcase with them into the doctor's laboratory. It was their bomb-detecting equipment, she said. One was fat and one was thin, too fat and too thin to be FBI men, she thought at first, but she had seen their metal badges so they had to be authentic, right?

Remo got her to promise she would say nothing about it to anyone. She must go home and rest. With an authoritative snap of his fingers, Remo pulled a patrol car over.

"She's in a state of shock," Remo said to the two patrolmen in the front seat, while guiding the woman into the rear. "Take her home."

"Shouldn't she go to a hospital for shock?"

"Not for this kind. C'mon, move it. There's been an explosion here. I'm going to speak to the chief right now."

The patrolmen, hearing the name that would absolve them of responsibility, drove away on a campus thoroughfare, and the chief of police, seeing an authoritative man in his thirties giving instructions to his own men, assumed that the man had some official standing. Especially when the man came over and assured him that nothing important had been damaged.

"Just some deaths, but damn, we were lucky. Incredibly lucky. Whole experiment in perfect shape. Incredible. Lucky."

Remo watched a rubber bag with the remains of the people who had been in the wrong room on the fourth floor being wheeled to an ambulance. The wheeling was a gesture of respect for the human dead. What was in the bags were body fragments only. Much of what had been in the laboratory would be sifted for evidence and if there were no complaints about missing pieces of relatives—as there rarely were in these situations—any miscellaneous ear or thumb might be just handily flushed down the toilet. Only the funeral homes would continue the myth.

"Where's the highest ranking college official here?" Remo asked. The chief pointed to a pudgy loaf of a man who stood by himself, looking up at the fourth floor and nodding as if a workman were explaining a building modification to him.

"Dean of students," said the chief.

"Right," said Remo. He thanked the chief and officiously moved through the crowd, telling everyone to step aside. The dean of students hardly noticed Remo. He appeared deep in thought.

"Everything's in good order. But keep it hush-hush."

"What's in good order?" asked the dean of students.

"Can't say," said Remo.

"No. Not government work. I hope this doesn't mean we're going to have another demonstration. It's been so quiet lately. I don't want another demonstration."

"One of your professors has been killed, hasn't he?"

"Yes. He had tenure," said the dean of students. Rather than ask what that meant, Remo moved on to the reporter in the gray suit.

"All right," he said. "This is a backgrounder. You can't quote me directly. All we lost were a few bodies. The project is in tip-top shape. Jeezus, we were lucky."

"The name of the project? How do you spell it?"

"That's classified. The name is classified. Just say it was a project of maximum high significance."

"That doesn't mean a frigging thing," said the reporter. Remo winked broadly.

"I'm going to quote a source saying that all we lost were lives. Do you want that?" asked the reporter.

"Fine," said Remo.

Going into the building, Remo was stopped by a fire inspector. But Remo pointed to the police chief, the chief waved back, and the fire inspector said, "You'll need a mask."

"I won't breathe," said Remo.

The inspector blinked in surprise and Remo went into the building. Firemen moved in the jerky manner of those accustomed to having to turn their masked faces to be able to see what was beside them. They wore their rubber coats which protected them from water but couldn't stop the heavy smoke from getting into their clothes. Remo turned into the first room and looked around in the dim gray smoke. He saw a desk at the front of the room and examined it for drawers. It had none.

All he needed was a box or a drawer or a file folder. Any one of those would do, but he couldn't find anything suitable. Nor was there anything in the next room or the next. Schools were not the same as he had remembered them, but as he passed a room marked "men," he knew something had to stay the same. People had to dry their hands, and towels or blowers had boxes.

The University of California at Berkeley, Remo discovered, used towels with the ancient admonition of "rub, don't blot." The box was painted white. Remo ripped it off the wall and chipped paint off it by twisting the metal, until the box was almost shiny. Then he took out the towels, held the empty box in his arms as if it were a baby, and left the building, pushing aside a stumbling nurse who was escorting a burn victim from the scene.

"Excuse me," said Remo.

He went through the crowd, past the fire inspector and the chief of police and the dean of students and the reporter, saying over and over again, "Not a scratch on it. Not a scratch on it. Beautiful. Not a scratch on it."

"Not a scratch on what?" asked the reporter, trying to get a glimpse of the cargo which Remo shielded with his arms. But Remo only winked and hurried across campus to the administration building, where he grandly announced he was going to "stay with it for the night because maybe the next explosion won't leave us all so lucky."

"Lucky?" asked a secretary, amazed to jaw-gaping disbelief. "Five people were killed, including a tenured professor."

"Yeah. Next time it could be serious," said Remo, and ordered the secretaries to show identification. When a man in a vest with a gold key dangling from it came into the office to ask what was going on, Remo demanded his identification too, and said he didn't like the idea of everyone hanging around this office without clearance and people casually coming in and out. He didn't know what others might do but he was going to stay here all night with it.

"With what?" asked the man with the gold key.

"You're a little bit too nosy for your own good. Out. All of you. Out. Goddamned petty bureaucrats. We luck out of this thing and you damned administrators have to go around screwing it up again. Five men are dead. Isn't that enough for you? Isn't five dead enough for you? Get the hell out of this office, all of you."

In a burst of generosity, Remo let the secretaries find their handbags and take them with them. But not their coats. Five persons dead already, you know. It was about time the University of California had some security.

By 5:30 P.M., as the sun began its red descent over the Pacific and Remo sat with the altered towel box in his lap in the administration building, the FBI came to check out what had been removed from the science building. The two men showed their shiny metal badges.

"Ah, Mobley and Philbin," said Remo. "You don't look like FBI men. You're odd-sized. And how come you have badges? The FBI uses ID cards."

"Special branch," said Mobley.

"Is that the thing the radio station was talking about?" asked the one named Philbin.

Remo nodded. "Made it myself," he said.

"You're not a scientist, are you?"

"No. I'm the man who's going to kill you," said Remo pleasantly. Mobley and Philbin quickly unholstered their guns. Philbin pointed the barrel of his at the wise guy's temple and strangely enough the guy watched only Philbin's trigger finger. As if he could dodge a bullet if he saw the finger begin to move. Philbin had never seen anything like that before. He had seen guys so close the brains had gone splooey out of their crushed skulls as the bullets set off little compression explosions until the temple popped, but never had he seen anyone whose eyes focused on the finger. They always looked at the barrel before they died. Not the finger. This close, no one had ever looked at Philbin's finger before.

Mobley searched the adjacent offices. Philbin kept the barrel pressed to the wise guy's temple.

Remo hummed a bar from "Whistle While you Work."

"No one here," said Mobley.

"He's just a wise guy," said Philbin.

"You're not FBI men," said Remo.

"We have the guns. We'll do the talking," said Mobley. "First of all, who are you?"

"I told you. The man who's going to kill you. Now if you're pleasant and polite, you'll have a nice departure. But if you're going to be nasty, it's going to hurt. Truly, I recommend the nice departure. It's like, now you're here and now you're not. Probably better than any death you could manage on your own. Even a fast heart attack isn't any pleasure."

"I find it hard to believe that my partner and I have guns pointed at your head and you're threatening us with death."

"But you've got to believe," said Remo earnestly. The very calmness of his voice had a rhythm that made people feel more at ease. Philbin saw the wise guy's head turn away, and suddenly felt a tearing burn at his trigger finger. He saw the automatic pop out of Mobley's large limp hand and he decided, as he had decided with Dr. Ravelstein, that he was not going to dally with death. He squeezed the trigger finger despite the pain and then he realized in screaming agony that from the joint of his thumb to his middle finger there were only a few dangling strands of flesh and the hand then didn't hurt anymore, and then it was dark. Forever.

Remo held up Mobley's head so he could watch Philbin's eyes roll to the back of his head in death.

"Who sent you?" asked Remo.

"I never saw him."

"Nonsense," said Remo.

"No. We never saw him. He was always in a shadow."

"How could he be in a shadow today? He had to send you back here."

"Yeah, yeah. He sent us. He sent us."

"And you didn't see him?"

"No. Never."

"Pretty dangerous making hits for someone you don't see."

"He paid well."

"Why didn't you rob him, or would that be against the law?"

"On him, no. He was crazy as hell."

"Where are you supposed to meet him next?"

"You're going to think this is crazy, buddy. But he said if anybody asked us that question, we should just tell him that he would have to wait. That's all he told us. That and he made us drink that funny sounding juice."

"Juice?" asked Remo.

"Yeah. It sounded something like tangerine juice."

Remo ignored that puzzle. "Why were you hitting the scientists?"

"I don't know."

"Which oil company were you working for?"

"You gotta ask the man. I don't know."

"Do you know the FBI doesn't use metal badges?" Remo asked.

"I know that. The crazy guy told us to use them."

"He's not so crazy. He told you to use them so I'd know you weren't FBI men. I'll tell you what. Get me to him and I'll give you your life. Your life for his."

Mobley laughed and the laughter became tears and the tears became a sigh and suddenly Mobley was losing body heat. He was dying. Remo felt the life slipping away under his hand.

Mobley's eyes began to glaze over.

Remo watched, then remembered. "That juice?" he said to Mobley. "Tangerine juice?"

"Sounded like that," said Mobley faintly.

"Could he have said 'Sinanju'?" Remo asked.

"Yeah. That was it. Sinanju," said Mobley, and then he fell from Remo's grip and died on the floor.

Remo looked down at the dead body. He took the useless gun from the man's disabled hand and put it back in the shoulder holster. He did not know why he did this, but it somehow seemed appropriate.

Then he walked out into the California sun. The two fake FBI men had been poisoned by the drink. They had been supposed to stay alive long enough so Remo would know who he was facing this time.

Well, they had, and he did.

He had been challenged again by Nuihc, the evil offspring of Sinanju and its mysterious arts.

CHAPTER FIVE

In the Grand Islamic Council of the Revolutionary People's Free Arab Republic, formerly Lobynia, Col. Muammar Baraka listened to the endless reports that had been typed in triplicate by British typists on German typewriters with electricity supplied by American generators run by Belgian mechanics.

The council met in the old king's palace, a building constructed by an Italian nobleman, designed by a Japanese architect, with American air conditioning, British wiring, Danish furniture, and East German flooring.

Lobynia's green and orange flag with the yellow crescent and star sometimes fluttered, but more often drooped in the windless heat. It had been made, designed, and manufactured in Lobynia by Lobynian technicians and was perfectly good except that it had to be replaced each week since the grommets through which the flag rope passed regularly fell out every seven days.

Baraka listened. Near his right hand was a Texas Instruments pocket calculator. Since he had become president four years before, he had written down on a little pad how much oil his country had in estimated reserves. On another pad, he estimated how much money was leaving the country. The amount of money leaving grew and grew, and soon needed electronic calculation. Estimated oil reserves shrank at a steady rate and remained on the same pad on which he had first written them down when he deposed King Adras. For the last four years, he thought about the difference every day. He thought about it when he watched the wing fall off a hangared Mirage jet because it had just rusted off. The hangar was too near the sea. A plane that never flew should not be hangared near the sea. He thought about the difference when the Russian-built office complex collapsed because of a combination of poor building materials and no maintenance. And he thought about it very strongly when he heard an Italian engineer explain to a Russian that anything built in Lobynia should need no more skill to operate than an oasis.

"But an oasis is just there," said the Russian.

"Ahhh," said the Italian. "Now you know how to build for the Lobynians. Unless you plan to have Russians in the country on permanent maintenance duty."

Colonel Baraka remembered this conversation as he watched his country's wealth being pumped from its sands, never to return again, and buildings crumbled and planes fell apart in their hangars and everyone wanted to sell him something because they were "friends of the Arabs."

"So when he heard even such a small expense as two hundred fifty thousand dollars American, he questioned it.

"What are the Lobynian people getting for this two hundred and fifty thousand dollars?"

"Colonel?" asked the Minister of Intelligence. He was almost as young as the Colonel, but his face had gotten fat and he had started to wear uniforms of expensive cloth from Britain. He had taken a promotion to lieutenant general after the revolution. It had been he who delivered the crucial armored corps at the crucial moment, namely the jeep that worked and could get Colonel Baraka to the radio station. In Baraka's voice, the people found a memory of strength and trust. It was his voice that was the revolution and his spirit was the light of the people. And all the officers sitting at the conference table in the palace knew it. They knew that they held their ranks by his word and by nothing else. Even the soldiers had to be told from time to time that it was the colonel's orders, before they did something. Now Lieutenant General Jaafar Ali Amin looked up from the long list of monthly intelligence expenses, amazement wrinkling his face and blanching a long white scar that ran down his left cheek.

"Colonel, I don't understand."

"I am asking," said Baraka, "what did we get for that two hundred fifty thousand dollars American? That's what I asked. What did the Lobynian people get that they can say this is what our leaders got for us with the fruits of our land?"

"Well, it's under the heading of American projects which is roughly twenty million dollars this month. That includes, I might add, financing student organizations in which we are picking up broad support far beyond investments, growing favor for our cause among minority groups in America, payments to friends and to that United States senator who on public television . . ."

"Wait. Hold it. Hold it. Spare me the list of your successes. Just tell me, specifically and unalterably and finally, what did we get for that two hundred and fifty thousand American dollars, eh?"

The colonel's sharp, Italian-looking features tightened in frustration as he spoke. His neck reddened.

"Incidentals. Two," said Lt. General Jaafar Ali Amin in an almost inaudible voice. He did not look up from the typed papers.

"Was that one hundred and twenty-five thousand dollars an incidental, or was one incidental two hundred thousand dollars and the other, being an even more incidental incidental, only fifty thousand dollars?" asked Baraka.

"It doesn't say, Colonel."

"Don't you know? Aren't intelligence operations in your department?"

"But, Colonel," said General Ali Amin, looking up from the paper at last. "In my budget, that amount is less than one one-hundredth. Do you know where every hundredth of something you spent has gone?"

"Yes," Baraka said. "Now you find out. I remember when outside this building there was not two hundred and fifty thousand dollars that belonged to the people of my tribe or my father's tribe or the tribe of his father's father."

"Things are different today, oh, leader, especially since you have led the way in raising world prices of oil four times higher than they had been before."

"Yes," said Baraka. His face broke into a sudden smile and his ministers smiled with him, largely in relief. "Now instead of a mere two hundred and fifty thousand dollars of incidentals we could for the same amount of oil leaving the land get one million dollars worth of incidentals." Baraka paused. The smiles disappeared around the table.

"Four times as much, gentlemen," Baraka said. "Now I will tell you what we will all do. We will all wait here until General Ali Amin finds out what has been done with the people's two hundred and fifty thousand dollars American."

"With exactitude," said the General. He saluted smartly and left, shutting the door behind him. Twenty minutes later, as the fingers drummed on a table surrounded by sheepish men and one man furious to the limits of his tether, General Ali Amin returned with a fat file folder in his hands and a confident smile on his face.

"The two incidentals, sir, went for a Mobley and a Philbin with the European capital letter 'T' on it. Exactly, Colonel," and he saluted again, put the paper back in the folder and sat down.

"Capital T, you said?"

"Yes, Colonel. A capital T exactly. Specifically. Just as exactly as the American shot to the moon."

"And would you mind telling us what this capital T means?"

"Sir?"

"Get the Frenchman."

"Sir?"

"The civilian aide who runs your whole department while you are out cornholing little boys in the streets of our capital. Yes, I know what you do."

General Ali Amin shrugged. His attempt at self-respect had failed in the face of the onslaught of reality. He summoned the Frenchman.

M. Alphonse Jaurin, a thin man with a dark ferretlike face and very precisely cut black hair, did not officially exist, although his services were rented from the French government for a sum that could have bought another Mirage jet to join the rusting fleet.

Not existing, M. Jaurin did not have a title. Not existing, he did not wear a uniform, but a dark pin-striped suit with a vest. And not existing, he went where he wanted without being bothered, except when Colonel Baraka wanted to find out what was happening. Then a messenger would run frantically to M. Jaurin's palatial home on Gamal Abdal Nasser Avenue searching for the small Frenchman. But today was the day of the ministers and like all the other foreigners who worked in subordinate roles in Lobynian ministries, he sat outside the main conference room in the palace. He was chatting with the Russian who had done interesting work in Czechoslovakia and was now in Lobynia as part of his nation's buildup in the Middle East. He had confided that the Russians needed the Arabs about as much as Americans needed the South Vietnamese.

M. Jaurin was surprised to see General Ali Amin return to the waiting room, anxious and flustered.

"He wants to see you," said the general.

"In person?" asked M. Jaurin.

"Yes. In person."

"But that's an official room. An official meeting. You know I am not supposed to be there. Never. It would be ... well, official."

"The colonel ordered."

"As he wishes, but you had better be right, Amin, or ... well, you had just better be right, or else."

"I am right. I am definitely right, M. Jaurin."

"We will see," he said and entered the main conference room as General Ali Amin opened the door for him and closed it behind him.

Colonel Baraka examined the man whose yearly salary could not have been borne by the entire income of the colonel's tribe a generation before, but was now a sum routinely spent on acquiring information about what other countries were doing. Colonel Baraka often judged this to be misinformation. The Frenchman's eyes were black, his skin pocked, and the hair precisely combed. Men with precise hair tended to hide things well.

"You're Jaurin and you run our intelligence service," said Baraka and saw Jaurin blink. The Frenchman did not expect this sort of truthfulness from an Arab.

"Well, I am an associate of a business firm with a license to to ..."

"Stop the nonsense. I hear too much of it. I called you in for some answers. What does the European 'T' mean?"

"Terminate, sir."

"Fire, kill, stop paying, what?"

"Kill, sir."

"We kill, they kill, who kills?"

"I assume it is the Mobley and Philbin terminations in America you are referring to. That was the file I sent for."

"From home, no doubt."

"Well, on occasion the air conditioning at the intelligence building . . ."

"Enough, Jaurin. You keep our intelligence files at home so they won't get lost and so you can clear everything with your own headquarters. I know what you do."

"Let me say, Colonel, that M. Jaurin has served Lobynia with a devotion, courage, and perseverance that . . ." started Ali Amin, but was interrupted by the sound of Baraka's hand slamming down on the table.

"Shut up. Shut up. Shut up," yelled Colonel Baraka. "Jaurin, where did my people's money go? For what?"

"I am glad you asked that, Colonel. I am especially glad you picked this small item. It illustrates the honor of France and the French people who love you and your Arab brethren. The money went for death benefits. Death benefits paid to the families of two men who were terminated while working in the glorious cause of Arab unity, Colonel. Men who died for Lobynia."

Lt. General Ali Amin stood slightly more erect, trying in some way to cadge some of the glory of the fallen dead. The council of ministers nodded solemnly. For a moment all were caught in the deep significance of the never-ending battle of international intrigue. One general suggested a moment of silence. Another proclaimed that neither Mobley nor Philbin died in vain, and would indeed live as long as any Arab could raise a gun for final vengeance, blood, and justice.

Only Colonel Baraka seemed unimpressed. He drummed his long fingers and M. Jaurin felt his palms become very wet, as they had the day he emerged from St. Cyr as a second lieutenant destined for Algeria where he became one of his nation's Arab experts, which was really what he was still doing in Lobynia—spying on it.

"Everyone but the Frenchman leave this room," said Baraka. The order was met by murmurs, until he slammed his open palm down on the table and there was a race for the door.

"Now, you insidious little French weasel, what the hell are we doing killing people in America?"

"I didn't say we killed someone. I said two of our men were terminated."

"I don't believe you, weasel. There has been talk in the diplomatic community about American scientists being killed to prevent the discovery of an oil substitute ... don't interrupt me, weasel ... let me draw you a little scenario." Colonel Baraka rose from the table, a trim, immaculately dressed man in light tan battle uniform. At his right was a polished black leather holster, containing a .38 caliber Smith and Wesson revolver. Baraka showed the revolver to Jaurin. Barrel first. He cocked the revolver. Jaurin looked at the barrel then at Baraka. He smiled wanly.

"Now, let me tell you what is happening. American scientists die. They do not produce a substitute for oil. America becomes more dependent on foreign imports, despite the price ... no, no. Don't interrupt. These things tend to go off when I am interrupted. Now, as America gets more dependent on imports, Arab power becomes greater. As Arab power becomes greater, French power vis-à-vis America becomes greater. But France doesn't want to risk responsibility for this, so why not have the crazy Lobynian leader, Colonel Baraka responsible. Eh?

Why not? Why we can even get that filthy wog to pay for it. Eh? Eh?"

"But, your excellency, that doesn't make sense. Why would France want to weaken the West? We are a Western nation."

"Because you are shortsighted idiots with the moral fiber of the surface of the Seine—scum to be exact. Yes, it is a stupid, shortsighted self-serving policy, which means it must be French. The very flavor is French. Like cheese. It has a French aroma. Yes. Kill American scientists with Baraka's money. And if a few assassins are killed along the way, why, pay off their families. Call it death benefits and the filthy wog will never even guess what is happening."

"If, excellency ... If, excellency, we are doing that, then don't you profit?"

"I profit right up until the United States of America traces the deaths to me. I profit right up until then, you little weasel. Now, you scummy little spy, I am ordering you on penalty of your life to call off that assassination mission."

"Certainly. Right now, your excellency. Immediately."

"You're not dealing with General Ali Amin now. I want to watch you write out the order. I want to know the exact chain to reach the operatives. I want to see it done."

"There is a little problem, your excellency. The operative who runs that American system contacts us; we don't contact him."

"Are you telling me we have an operative running around a nation with nuclear power, killing its top scientists, losing his own men in the process and we cannot even reach him? Is that what you're telling me, Jaurin? Is that what you're telling me? I'd like to know."

"Could you lower that gun, your excellency?"

"No."

"We tried calling him off. He had a postal drop. We didn't even want the second scientist killed. But it got out of hand. We couldn't reach him. And then the second one was killed. Finally he did contact us. I personally told him to stop. He said he could not stop because it was not time yet to stop."

"Then why did you pay the death benefits for Mobley and Philbin? If the man was disobeying your orders?"

"That was strange, excellency. He told me they were going to have accidents and he wanted the money. When I refused to pay, he said it would be terrible if they talked and told that they were working for the . . Lobynian government. So we paid. And a third scientist was killed, and Mobley and Philbin were killed, too."

"I am glad to see that Lobynia does not have a monopoly on incompetence. Why did you hire this nut?"

"He came to us with the proposal. It seemed very carefully thought out. And we learned he was capable of doing it because he comes from a tradition of assassins. The finest assassins in the world. That is why we did it."

"No. You hired this nut whom you can not control because if anything went wrong, I would be blamed. The Duixeme, your intelligence, would never have an operative it could not call off. Oh, no, that would be too risky for the French. But not for the crazy Lobynian leader. One can do anything in his name."

"That's not true."

"The Islamic law is the law of our land. We cut off the hands of people who steal. For people who lie to chiefs, we cut out tongues."

"Your excellency, I will serve you instead of France. Let me serve your greatness. I deny Christ for Allah, your excellency. Look at me on my knees. I am getting on my knees. In the name of Allah, I beg your mercy. You cannot refuse this plea."

"Good. Since Islam is the one true faith, I now send you in glory to Allah," said Colonel Baraka and pulled the trigger. There was a loud bang, and the white forehead snapped back as though it were on a pulley. The bullet made a dark red hole above the nose and took off the back of the head, spraying dark reddish brain on the rug and chairs. Then Baraka put the gun back in his holster, opened the conference room door and invited back his ministers and their foreign aides.

"Here. Come in here and look. See what happens to him who tries to risk the lives of my people. Come. Come in here when you think you can play with the lives of my people like so many pawns."

Soon the colonel left them and went out into the desert, which really began at the shacks that marked the outskirts of the capital city. He rode a white horse, and guided it miles away to a watering place his people had known for many generations. There he prayed, begging guidance from Allah. He went to sleep, thinking of the wealth beneath the ground and how it kept diminishing and all he had for it were planes that rusted, buildings that collapsed, and assassin lunatics who might get all his people killed. He had tried. No one could dispute that he had tried. He had tried to make the Army efficient but it still resembled a girl scout troop, except that girl scouts had more discipline. He had tried to make the economy work, but an economy would not work unless the people worked, and he had not found the secret yet to make that happen. He had tried to interest Egypt in a merger of the two countries with Egypt supplying brains and Lobynia supplying money, but Egypt had responded with speeches that were really patronizing pats on the head. Oh, if only Nasser were still alive.

Baraka thought these things and finally fell asleep, only to dream of the revolution four years before. He awoke suddenly because he heard old King Adras's voice repeat that foolish prophecy designed to enslave the peasants. He looked around and he saw that he was alone. The king was not there. Perhaps it had been the talk of assassins that made him think he heard the prediction over again. The king was gone. There was a new government, this one dedicated to the people's welfare. In the old days, the king took all the wealth and let the oil companies even ruin the watering holes, leaving nothing and giving nothing back to the people.

He thought of this and remembered how he had gotten so many officers to follow him. He had taken them to an important oasis and bade them drink. The water tasted waxy from the refuse of crude oil.

"Lo, I say unto you. Your sons and their sons will be denied good water. For taking out oil destroys the water. I say unto you King Adras will allow us to be left without water. We must force the oil companies to take oil in such a way as to leave water for our sons."

After the revolution was successful, the first thing Baraka did as president was to call in all oil company presidents and lay down the first of his unalterable laws.

"You shall not take water from my people. You shall not make our water unfit to drink."

As one, the oil company presidents rose and swore to keep the water pure at all costs. Later, Baraka found these costs were deducted from royalties per barrel paid to Lobynia.

But it was only money. No matter. So he had not straightened out the economy, the armed forces, the health problems, the illiteracy. If he had done nothing else but preserve the water for the future, he was doing more than any other ruler had ever done. He was doing what a good chief must do for his people. It made him feel satisfied.

Colonel Baraka went to the watering hole and on his

knees lowered his hands into the dark water, watching the moon's yellow reflections on its surface. The water felt cool from the deep spring that was its source. He felt the water soak the knees of his trousers, and that was good. How could a Bedouin tell anyone else how good water felt. Impossible to tell. But it was water and it was good. It was good to get down on your knees to drink.

He put his face into the little pool and drank deeply, feeling reassured. Until he tasted it. The water was waxy. And for the first time, Colonel Baraka wondered how King Adras liked Switzerland, and whether he might enjoy it there himself.

CHAPTER SIX

The bodies of Mobley and Philbin were claimed by two black-garbed, grieving widows. The smell of their perfume was so overpowering that the FBI agents questioning them tried to breathe without taking in any of the surrounding air. It wasn't easy. They retched every once in a while, but finally the women agreed to go outside the city morgue with them and talk downwind.

Well, they weren't *exactly* wives, the two women said. They had been hired by this guy they hadn't seen. He gave them money and told them to claim the bodies.

"You met him where?" asked one of the agents.

"At work," said the one whose hair was the yellow of bad lemon candy. Her lipstick was thick red paste, glistening under her black veil. The heavy ropy eyelashes touched the veil on every blink. The agent estimated her age at thirty to fifty, give or take ten years.

"Where do you work," asked the agent. He heard his partner snicker.

"Kansas City," said the woman. "Kansas City, Kansas."

"What kind of business I meant."

"Exotic massage and body counseling."

"I see. Tell me more about this man who hired you. Was he tall, short? What?"

"What would you say, Carlotta?" asked the blonde.

"He was about average for a short kind of guy. You know?"

"No. Is that five-ten, five-seven, what?"

"You know, come to think of it, I didn't get a good look at him. He was like shorter. Maybe five-two, I guess."

"How can a man appear average and be five-two?" asked the agent.

"It was strange, he sort of moved in shadows."

"What color hair?"

"Black. I think he was Japanese."

"No. No, remember," said the blonde. "Somebody said Japanese and he said Korean. Remember?"

"What did he want you to do with the bodies?"

"Well, that's the strange part. He said we'd never have to worry about bringing them anywhere. Just claim them and say, what was it, Carlotta, both fat and thin."

"Yeah, that was it," Carlotta agreed exuberantly, as if she were solving everything. "Fat and thin."

"Well, we done our part," said the blonde.

The FBI did not detain the two women. They added the obscure conversation to a growing list of peculiarities about Mobley and Philbin, two Kansas City hoods whose descriptions fit the men who had been seen leaving Ravelstein's office, going into the science building at Berkeley before it blew up, and leaving Rensselaer Polytech just before Dr. Erik Johnson took a header down a stairwell.

The murders had all been well planned and executed. The work was certainly not sloppy. But why then had they carried metal badges? That was sloppy; anyone could find out that the FBI carried identification cards.

And the way they had died was strange. At a meeting with some unknown man, Philbin with half his hand ripped off, and Mobley by some unknown poison. And who was the unknown man?

They had no answers. They put all the questions in their reports. When they considered how crucial the energy shortage was, the two real FBI men were stunned when the case appeared to have been dropped.

"Sir, we don't understand."

"We have our orders. I imagine another bureau is handling it."

The FBI men shrugged. It must be international, a project for the CIA. Over at the CIA in Langley, Virginia, those concerned thought the FBI was handling it.

And everyone was satisfied, except for a man in a small office facing Long Island Sound—Dr. Harold Smith, the head of the secret agency CURE. He was handling the case and he was stumped.

He walked from his office down to the small wharf at the back of the Folcroft Sanitarium grounds. It was evening and it was dark across Long Island Sound. The case had too many questions in it. At first he had thought a foreign country was behind the assassinations. Then he had changed his mind and decided that one of the big American oil companies was probably financing the killings. Either might still be correct.

But why the FBI badges? That was stupid—almost as if whoever was running the killings had wanted Mobley and Philbin to be unmasked as fakes. And what of the nonsense of "fat and thin"? What did that mean? It nudged something deep inside his brain, but he could not remember what it was.

Mobley was fat and Philbin was thin. Fat and thin. Apart from that, they were two ordinary small-time hoods with sudden skills and competence.

And Remo had found out nothing from them before they died.

57

Smith smelled the salt of the sound and felt the cooling moisture bathe his face. Who was behind it?

The Arab states? Estimates eliminated most of the large oil producers, and the wild man of the region, Colonel Baraka, who one day wanted to merge with Egypt and the next day with Tunisia and the next start a holy war against Israel, well he wouldn't dare conduct assassinations in America. Or would he?

But there were the oil companies. There was definite proof that an oil company had promised Arab states it would deny fuel to the American army. And hadn't they, from the outset of the oil squeeze, rigged prices to gouge the American public? It had been the oil companies that had begun the crippling price increase, even before the Arabs had started slowing down oil to America to make the increases even more crippling.

If there was an industry in America with a chilling contempt for American citizens, it was the oil industry. From the oil-soaked corpses of little birds washed up on scum-coated California beaches, to the multimillion-dollar propaganda that came out of New York City agencies, spent to convince the suffering that the oil companies were good guys, there was blatant disregard for the welfare of the world.

Millions were spent on misleading advertisements indicating that most of the oil was supplied by the Middle East, while the American oil companies actually had enough stored in Venezuela to keep America flooded for years. Tankers laden with oil lined up just outside the harbors, while children groped their way to school in the dark, because walking safely in the light would cost a few extra drops of oil. Walking safely in daylight meant a different time system that a country starved for oil could not afford. And the tankers waited out in the ocean for prices to go up a little more. Tankers filled and bobbing low in the water waited while American mothers buried their children who were killed walking to school in the dark.

And to counteract the growing rage, oil companies ran more advertisements implying that foreign policy was responsible for the shortage of oil—though if they got a rise in price, why then, all of a sudden, the oil worries would be over. And by the way, explained the public relations newspaper ads, the oil companies have record profits this year only because last year wasn't good enough; just look at the millions we spend for public commitment ...

The millions spent, the public relations ads did not mention, were for the public relations ads themselves. One could not turn on a television set at night without seeing fairy tales about what a public benefit the oil companies were. Why, birds and fish, if you were to believe the ads and commercials, just couldn't live without those wonderfully clean and cosmetic wells sunk into the belly of the earth that the animals—in fact, everyone—has to live on.

Dr. Smith thought about this, thought about workers laid off from their jobs and children dying in the darkness and the oil companies willing to sell out the nation's armed forces, and he knew the oil companies also might be behind the murders of the scientists.

A foreign country? Our own oil companies? He just didn't know enough to even guess. And gnawing at him was the mystery of fat and thin, and the two old whores who remembered someone probably Korean was paying them to claim two bodies. Why had to he done that? Obviously to send some kind of message. Probably that he was a Korean. But to whom was the message directed?

For the first time in many years, Smith was defeated. He had nothing. Nothing except Remo and Chiun, and he had no target to turn them loose against.

He thought again of the young children killed in the

predawn darkness and he decided to turn Remo loose. Find out what he could and stop what he could. It was all Smith had right now.

But when Smith reached out for his best shot again, it was not he who had his hand on the trigger.

CHAPTER SEVEN

Colonel Baraka discovered the real employer of the two hundred and fifty thousand dollar incidentals—two, with a capital European T, on a night that gave him more horror than he had ever felt in his four years as president of Lobynia. He felt as helpless as the day he had discovered that the French had secretly sold the latest engines for the Mirage to Israel and had shipped him the old ones. The Revolutionary People's Free Arab Republic had purchased the new Mirage jet bodies but not the engines. Baraka's air minister had assured him that it would not matter because the people would never know. Colonel Baraka hanged his air minister quietly, in an unused hangar, and did not tell the people that their new planes were inadequate to bomb Tel Aviv the next day.

But this was the new night of his helpless horror. Out of his entire army, Baraka had found fifty men who would serve as commandoes to make secret night strikes inside Israel. They had completed their training and were now to undergo night exercises, a secret assault against caves outside the capital city of Dapoli which were like those in the Judean hills. The French ambassador was there with Baraka to see how the Jews would be slaughtered. For the exercises, these slaughters would be simulated, of course, since the last few Jews who had lived in Lobynia had either escaped the country or had their throats cut by screaming mobs. The colonel had remembered the black writer who, when he met an Arab in Tel Aviv whose running water did not always function well, commented that he knew what it was like to be an Arab at the hands of the Jews, the implication being that he didn't like Jewish landlords.

"He should try being a Jew at the hands of an Arab," laughed one of the colonel's cabinet and Baraka had smiled. As prizes from the last war the Arabs had lost, his cabinet had noses and ears from Israeli prisoners of war that had been presented as gifts from Iraqi, Syrian, and Moroccan soldiers. When Colonel Baraka had been offered a nose, he had slapped the Syrian ambassador.

"Do you think the Jews will fight less hard after this useless butchery, you fool?"

Later he had commented that he knew the Islamic cause would triumph because "all the human excrement is on our side. We will always have them outnumbered."

Now searchlights played along the dry caves outside Dapoli and the commandoes weaved their way among the rocks. A general announced the plan for the mock attack. The set was this: the Israeli government had fled from Tel Aviv. Trapped in the caves, Golda Meir, Moshe Dayan, and General Sharon were begging for mercy. If they were not given mercy, they would wipe out Mecca with an atomic rifle provided by the pig United States.

This was the scene set through the scratchy megaphones in the sandy black night under the clearest sky the French ambassador said he had ever seen. Gray forms climbed up the sides of the rocks, ropes lowered, men grunted. The general explained through the megaphone that the exercise problem was to get the Jews before they destroyed Mecca with their atomic rifle. A surprise attack.

"But, Colonel," said the French ambassador, sipping an overly sweet almost almond-tasting soft drink because alcohol was outlawed in Lobynia, "if you had the Israeli cabinet trapped in the caves, wouldn't your war of extermination be complete? Why would you have to pursue them?"

"I don't want to exerminate the Jews or even eliminate Israel, if you must know the truth. The best thing we've ever had has been Israel and the best thing they've ever had has been us."

"I don't understand. With all due respect, Colonel, why does Israel need the Arabs?"

"Because without us, they would have a civil war within five minutes. There would be factions within factions within factions, and rabbis would stone socialists who would shoot at generals who would shoot everybody else. Mark me, the Jews are a contentious people and the only thing that holds them together is the threat of extermination. This is true."

Seeing the stunned look on the ambassador's face and not knowing whether it was because of the simulated screams from the caves, Baraka continued, "Hitler created the state of Israel and we keep it going. Without Israel, the word Arab would hardly be used. It would be Egyptian, Kuwaiti, Hashemite, Sunni, Lobynian. But not Arab. That is why, while we still have Israel as our unifying force, I want to merge countries. If peace with Israel should break out tomorrow, you could kiss the Arab cause good-bye. We would never advance technologically or socially. Never. All of us as peoples are doomed without Israel to fight."

The ambassador smiled broadly. "You are very wise, Colonel."

"To be wise, Mr. Ambassador, is merely not to be as

stupid as everyone else. That was what our king said to us, but he was a fool and now we have no king."

"That's not a Lobynian statement, you know," said the French ambassador, "and it's surprising that the saying should reach here. According to some French royalty, there was a house of assassins who . . ."

Suddenly a pitiful shriek came from one of the illuminated caves. The colonel and the ambassador were seated on the back of a flatbed truck with other dignitaries, holding their almond-flavored drinks. Their talking ceased, making the scream sound even more piercing in the abruptly silent night that smelled of the fumes of parked trucks and newly oiled weapons of war.

The caves were less than seventy-five yards away and they could see clearly a commando, his arms apparently tied behind his back, spin into the entrance of the cave. His shriek became a loud moan and then the moan became a pitiful little sob which did not stop. No one moved and everyone saw why it appeared from the front as if his hands were tied behind him. Spinning around in delirium, he showed all of them that this hands weren't in the back either. Someone had cut his arms off.

There was silence and then Colonel Baraka ordered doctors up to the man and a hundred voices were shouting orders.

"Aargh." Another moan filled the night as another commando crawled to the entrance of the cave and stopped. Then there was a groan, and nothing. A head came rolling out of the cave like a leather-bound melon and bounced down the Lobynian basalt and it was then that everyone realized that the second man who had crawled out of the supposedly empty caves had no legs.

"Attack, attack," yelled the commander of the Islamic commandoes before he ducked behind a searchlight. Everyone else took cover, until someone started firing at the cave and then the desert opened up in an explosion of automatic and semiautomatic weapons that whined into the cave and plastered the rocky rise, killing another half-dozen of their own commandoes.

When it was over, when the last pistol plinked away in the night, when the colonel had smacked enough soldiers in the back of the head and kicked enough behinds to stop them from making asses of themselves in front of foreigners by dissipating their ammunition like unseasoned troops, it was discovered that fifteen of their number had been killed by mutilation. And not by a knife, because a knife sharp enough to sever joints did not leave stringy strands of flesh.

Quickly, the mutilated were loaded into the ambulance that had accompanied the exercises for effect, presumably to take the bullet-riddled bodies of Golda Meir, Moshe Dayan, and General Sharon to the nearest garbage dump. But now the ambulance, which contained no medical equipment because someone had forgotten to load it, was to carry real Arab commandoes to the hospital.

"Like a bird with swiftness, oh driver, carry our brave fallen comrades to glory and to Dapoli," cried the commander. Seeing that the lazy driver had fallen asleep again, he ran—his feet sinking into the soft white sand—to the macadam road where he found the driver was not sleeping after all.

His head was tilted over his chest; his neck had been snapped. Pinned to his shirt was a note in an envelope.

The envelope said: "To be opened only by Colonel Baraka."

The note was delivered to Baraka, who did not open the envelope but had a jeep driver take him back to the capital alone. Everyone else stayed in a large group, their weapons drawn. They did not leave until dawn, and then only in a long convoy that started off slowly but ended with vehicles racing in a disorganized string on the road to the capital that cut a black line through the arid wasteland.

Back in the old king's palace, Colonel Baraka read the note many times. Then he took off his military uniform and, wearing the burnoose of his father and his father's father, got into a British land rover and headed out into the desert.

Out deep into the desert, the colonel drove, past the giant oil depots far to the left, where all Lobynia's oil eventually wound up for distribution, and then south along an uninterrupted black macadam line, a road that was always soft from the flat hot sun of the day. The sand was uninterrupted by a farm, by a home, by a factory. Not even a tree interrupted this land.

And yet the colonel knew that should one foreigner make this land fertile, plant one tree, drill and find water, plant and harvest a crop, there would be a national outcry, especially because the foreigner had done what Lobynians couldn't. Good, thought the colonel. If there were only some way he could plant another Israel closer to home. Work on his people's jealousy. Look what Israel had done for Egypt. It had goaded them into performing its first halfway competent military action since the defeat of the Hittites thousands of years before Christ. But if Egypt had erased Israel, Egypt would have returned to slumber.

From competence in military life would come competence in industry and in farming. It was Lobynia's only hope. And he, Colonel Baraka, was the only man who could bring it about. Without conceit or vanity he recognized this as simple truth. It was necessary, therefore, that he stay alive, and that was why he now drove into the desert.

So imperceptibly that one had to look far ahead and be

on one of the many small rises to realize it, the road curved. It was really a constant curve, but such was the desert and the human eye that the road appeared straight with a curve at the very end.

It was still dark as Baraka's rover slowly changed direction around the curve. On his right were what his people called the Mountains of the Moon. Foreigners had given them a Latin name, and thus the world knew the mountains as it wished to know them. But Baraka knew them differently; he had been lost there once as a young officer.

He had stumbled into a mountain tribe and had given food in exchange for directions. Nothing was free in these mountains.

When he gave more food, the wise man of the tribe had insisted upon giving "an extra direction" for the extra food. A prophecy. But, said the wise man, the prophecy would take some time to deliver. Baraka must wait for it.

Baraka had politely excused himself and left. The directions had proved accurate.

Years later, a ragged boy had appeared at a late night barracks meeting.

Baraka had heard a scuffle outside the tent where a meeting of military leaders was being held. He ran outside, pistol in hand. A guard was wrestling with a boy. When the colonel demanded to know what the fuss was about, the guard explained that one of the mountain people had gotten into the barracks area. The guard was trying to contain the boy, while keeping his nose as far away from him as possible.

Baraka could see that the boy's face was dirt caked and his hands and feet were black with travel. And the travel this boy had made, marked deep in his face, would subtract many a year from the far end of his life.

"A message, oh, Baraka. A message. For the extra food, an extra direction," cried the boy.

Baraka ordered the guard to release him. The boy fell to his knees to kiss the colonel's feet but Baraka raised him to his feet.

"Someday this will be a land where no man will kiss another man's feet," Baraka said. The generals had now emerged from the tent behind him and were looking at the boy. One whispered to another and then they all knew. This was the boy from the tribe of prophecy. One general said he was happy to see such a dirty creature, because at least everyone knew he wasn't from King Adras; everyone who served the king dressed well.

"Oh, Baraka, this then is the prophecy repaid unto you over these many years for the sustenance you gave."

"Speak, boy," said Baraka.

"Oh, Baraka, move tonight, for your enemy's wings are filled with the wine of destruction and you shall sit upon the great throne."

The generals hushed their conversation. How could anyone have known they were in the tent planning a revolution against King Adras?

Baraka looked at the boy. Finally, he said, "I will sit in no throne. I will not rule this land. But I will serve it."

One of the generals snorted a contemptuous laugh, noting the convenient timing. Baraka had been arguing for an immediate revolution; many of the generals had wanted to wait. And now this prophecy came, saying immediate revolution. Had the colonel ever really been lost in the mountains? he wondered.

A blood rage seized Baraka, and even as he drew his pistol to shoot the laughter off the face of the general, he knew that this time his rage served his good fortune, though this was usually just the opposite in others.

Baraka fired one shot into the mouth, and squeezed the second off at the nose. It caught the falling general in the right eye, which popped like a blood-filled balloon.

"Those who are not with me are against me," Baraka snarled, and thus that night the military took over the Lobynian government. What else could they do except follow a man who had a gun and was willing to risk his life, particularly while the king was in Switzerland with an air force chief of staff he wouldn't risk flying with.

When the king had not returned, the people's revolution was secure. A secret joke in some circles said that a man named Callahan from Jersey City had done more to change the history of the Middle East with a bottle of Seagram's Seven than all the Mirage jets that ever took off. Which was none of them.

That had been four years ago. It had been, Baraka remembered, a hot night, unlike tonight; he shivered in the open vehicle. He drank from a flask of water. Its warmth tasted good to him. At a large stone marker, he turned right. He had ordered this road built, ostensibly to create a gigantic religious crescent, but actually to give the mountain tribe an easier way to travel to Dapoli. He did not want such a journey to be a toll on one young boy's life again. To the best of his knowledge, no members of the mountain tribe had ever set foot on the road.

The land rover bumped across the rock and sand. It felt good to be out of the endless smooth hum of the main highway.

Fifteen miles along a very dry wash, wet perhaps twice a year, he felt something jump into the slow bouncing rover, grab him by the neck, and jerk him from the wheel. When he landed he could not stand up. His legs were numb from sitting for hours. He felt a rifle touch the temple of his head and someone took his pistol. He smelled the exhaust of the land rover that stood idling in the sand.

"Do not move, European pig," said a voice above him. When he turned his head to see who had said such a thing, he felt the muzzle of the gun press it down again into the dirt.

"I am Bedouin, Arab," said Baraka. "I am son of Bedouin and grandson of Bedouin, for ages upon ages and generation upon generation."

"You look like European. Italian."

"I am not. Not one drop of Italian blood," said Baraka hopefully. "I come searching for the wise man."

"There are many wise men."

"The one who calls himself Baktar."

"Baktar is dead these many years. Fifteen years is Baktar dead."

"That is impossible. Just four years ago he sent me a prophecy in payment for food."

"Oh. You are that one. Come with me."

Baraka felt the gun go from his head. He rose unsteadily in the light of the moon upon the rocky hillside that was part of what his people called the Mountains of the Moon, but the world called the Mountains of Hercules. He was led up a path and was surprised to see women scurry around his rover like so many desert bugs, carrying away blankets, a rifle, a bandolier, the canteens. No one bothered to turn off the engine. He knew then that these people would just leave his vehicle running until it was out of gas. He, Colonel Muammar Baraka, would die because he ran out of gas on a road that was built over billions of barrels of it. It was unthinkable.

Unthinkable, hell. It would probably happen. True, there was a gigantic spare tank along with the extra large rover tank, but still not enough to let it waste. He might be left with barely enough to get back to the main road. In the one hundred and thirty degree daytime heat of Lobynia, that would be the same as barely dying.

"Let me go back and turn off my car's engine."

"You go back nowhere. You go ahead. Up. Move."

"Please, I will reward you. I will give you a great reward."

"Up. Move. Up."

And Muammar Baraka, whom the world thought ruled this land, climbed upward along the sharp rocks that cut his knees and hands. His captor seemed to lope with ease up these very cliffs that were so hard for him to climb. He realized that man not only does not rule land, he does not own it, but is a transient creature across its surface. Countries were not made from borders, but from people acknowledging some sort of common bond.

He was brought to a small fire, golden in the moon-washed chilly night. A man in rags, for these people lived in rags, sat before the fire and motioned the president of the nation to sit.

"Four years you govern this land, Muammar, and yet you come here in terror, do you not?" the man said.

"Yes. I seek further direction."

"And what do you give us in exchange?"

Muammar Baraka smelled a strange odor, and then he realized that the fire was burning dried animal droppings. The whole encampment reeked of human filth. He was used to air conditioning now and showers and cars and telephones. The Europeans had captured him, just as surely as if they put him in a cage. They had captured his soul, as they must have captured many a soul in this land. If he should live, he would outlaw electricity and ice cubes and air conditioning, except, of course, for hospitals. He would allow it in hospitals. And the world would call him crazy again, as they had when he had outlawed alcohol, reinstituted cutting off hands for thievery, forced women to wear the barakan again—the long sheetlike garment that covered everything but one eye.

He had done these things, and still the oil under the land flowed out and his people had not changed and he was their leader and he sat captive on a rocky hillside in the Mountains of the Moon which would still, in another hundred years when the oil was gone, be called the Mountains of Hercules and his people would still burn animal droppings to keep warm.

"What do you give us in exchange?" the old man repeated.

"I have built you a road to Dapoli. For you have I had this road built. No longer will it take months for you to reach the capital."

"When they were laying down the smooth blackness, it was good. There were things we could steal from the workers but now they are gone. The road means nothing."

"You can get to Dapoli in hours now instead of months."

"If you have a car."

"I will send you cars."

"You need gas for cars. We have no gas."

"I will send you gas."

"Will you send us fatted sheep?"

"I will send you fatted sheep."

"Rams or ewes? Of what number?"

"Of hundreds," said Baraka, annoyance rising in him as if this were another ministers' meeting.

"How many hundreds?"

"Three hundred," snapped Baraka.

"Of the three hundred, how many ewe and how many ram?"

"Three hundred of each. Now get to my problem. I need a direction."

"From whom will you steal these sheep?"

"Never mind, I'll buy them." But then, knowing the suspicious mind of his captors, he added, "From money we get from oil that comes out of the ground."

"You will steal it from the ground, then. All right. For

we know you, Muammar, and we have heard of your tribe, and you have never earned anything in all your lives. Knowing you have done nothing for this money, we believe you."

"This night I have received a note," Baraka said. He drew the note from a pocket and opened it in front of the dim flames from the fire. "It reads 'You face the death of the prophecy. Only I can save you.'" He looked up at the old man.

"So? What is your worry, if you have a champion?"

"Whoever he is, he kills in a most horrible way."

"Then you should be happy."

"I do not want around me someone who kills so many, just to say hello. And what is the death of the prophecy?"

"Did you not depose King Adras?"

"Yes."

"Did he not tell you of the assassin's curse?"

"Yes."

"Well, then, you are about to pay the price for stealing the kingdom from a descendant of the great Caliph. This story is very old and we of the mountains have known it, surely you in your city which has horses and horses and horses of great beauty should know it. Your city has silks and sweet drinks and you should know it. Why do you not know it?"

"But that story was just a story. Why should I now pay the price?"

"Why not now? Did the curse say you would lose your life the day you took the crown? In the season you took the crown? In the year you took the crown?"

"No," said Baraka and his voice was hollow and flat. He waited, looking at the campfire. He realized he was hungry, but when he asked for food he was refused.

"The blessed Mohammed never lived in the Mountains of the Moon. But I will give you something of his before you leave. He said, and it is written, that a tiger cannot be anything but a tiger. That a chicken can never be anything but a chicken. Only a man has a choice. He can be a beast or a man. Go now, for we are afraid of you here. You carry a curse on your head."

"I will not leave until you shed light on your sayings."

"You will meet death from the East but it comes from the West. Nothing can save you. Go, before you bring death to others."

Baraka was led back to his land rover, which was still idling on the last dregs of the first tank. He put the car into reverse and began backing out of the wash when the tank ran dry. He switched to the emergency tank, but the switch did not work. He looked for a flashlight; it was gone. The beams of his headlights began to dim. He looked for a canteen the women of the tribe might have missed, but they was gone. He turned off the lights and crawled under the rover. Perhaps he could activate the second tank by hand. Or even siphon the reserve tank into the first one. His head hit the grease-and-sand-coated tank as he slid between rock and undercarriage. It made a hollow sound. Colonel Muammar Baraka who had been harassing the industrialized nations of the world by jacking up the price of their oil, was out of gas. And in the Mountains of the Moon, he began to realize what it was like to be out of gas and cold.

He cursed the tribe that had left him stranded, and then he heard a strange voice.

"Do not blame them. They were frightened. There has been a mysterious apparition here, waiting for you." The voice was squeaky and high-pitched.

Baraka struggled out from under the rover. He looked around the barren rocks, bright in the light of the full moon, but he saw no one. Then he heard the voice again.

"You are such a fool, Baraka, such a fool. Do you

think you can escape what is written by running back here? I tell you, Colonel, I am the only one who can save you."

"Are you the one who killed my commandoes?"

"Yes."

"Are you the one who wanted death payments for Philbin and Mobley?"

"Yes."

"Why do you want to protect me?"

"I don't, really. Your life is nothing to me. Important to me is a white pig I have awaited. And also he who gave away the precious secrets to the white man. I await them both."

"Are they of the legend?"

"We all are."

"Oh," said Colonel Baraka, his mind already made up. He would do anything, pay any price, to be protected. Legends need not always be true. He waited a moment, then said, "I hope, if you're going to keep me alive, that you have a way out of here."

"I do. Go up that little rise and there are several cans."

"How did you get out here? Where is your vehicle?"

"Never mind that. Move, wog."

"Help me with the cans."

"You will fetch, Colonel. For you are good for little else. Neither womb, nor wealth he has not earned is the measure of a man, but what he has been trained to do. Only his skills are his worth. You are fit for little more. Fetch."

And as the voice had said, there were cannisters of gasoline. The supposed ruler of the land filled the rover's tanks, and as he backed out of the wash a frail figure glided into the seat next to him. The figure chuckled and placed the colonel's own revolver on the colonel's lap. When the rover had reached the highway again and the way was smooth, the colonel got a good look at the face of the man who sat beside him. He was Oriental and fragile-looking. The hair was black and straight and long, and the smile seemed almost gracious.

With one hand, Baraka gripped the handle of his revolver. He pointed it at the smiling face.

"Never call me wog again," said Baraka, anger mounting in his throat.

"Put the gun away, wog."

Baraka squeezed the trigger. The barrel flashed bright white. The colonel blinked away the bright spot which remained in his sight but he could not blink away that smiling face. It was still there. Somehow the point blank shot had missed.

"I told you to put the gun away, wog."

"Please don't call me that."

"A 'please' is a different thing, wog. I will think about it. You might as well know the name of your new master. I am called Nuihc. You are the bait for my trap. You and your savage nation's oil. The oil is very important. Much more than you are."

"What about the oil?" asked Baraka.

"Tomorrow you will turn it off. You will sell no more."

CHAPTER EIGHT

Chiun's interminable afternoon with the soap operas had finally ended. He rose from his lotus position and turned, all in the same fluid motion, and looked toward the far wall of the hotel room, where Remo was exercising.

Chiun, as was his habit, left the television on. Turning it off was servant's work, fit only for Chinese or students. Remo would do it later.

Remo was upside down against the far wall, but he was not touching it. His feet pointed toward the ceiling, his arms were fully extended and he held himself up on his two index fingers.

He raised his head awkwardly and saw Chiun.

"How's this, Chiun?" he called.

"Try it on one finger," Chiun said.

Remo slowly shifted the balance of his weight until his body was directly over his right index finger. Then he lifted his left hand off the floor.

"Hah? Hah?" he called triumphantly. "How about that, Little Father?"

"There is a man in your circus who can do that. Now bounce."

"Bounce?"

"Yes. Bounce on your finger."

"All right. If you say so," Remo said. He tensed the tendons of his wrist, then relaxed them slightly. His body lowered imperceptibly over his hand. Then he snapped the tendons into tightness. The sudden expansion raised him by inches. He did it again and again, faster and faster. On the fourth try, the upward momentum of his body pulled his right index finger an inch off the floor.

He came back down on the index finger. It held, but wavered a moment, and the slight wavering tossed him off balance. His feet hit the wall, rebounded, and he fell softly into a ball on the rug.

He looked sheepishly toward Chiun, but Chiun's back was turned to him, again looking at the television.

"I fell, Chiun," Remo said.

"Shhhh," said Chiun. "Who cares?"

"But I fell. What did I do wrong?"

"Be born," Chiun said. "Be quiet. I am listening to something."

Remo got to his feet and went to stand alongside Chiun, whose attention was riveted on the six o'clock news.

The announcer's crisp voice was saying: "In announcing the cutoff of Lobynian oil to the United States, President Baraka said it was in retribution for this nation's continued support of Israel."

Chiun looked to Remo. "Who is this Baraka?"

"I don't know," Remo said. "The president or something of Lobynia?"

"What happened to King Adras?"

"Adras? Adras?" Remo thought. "Oh yeah, he was deposed. By Baraka."

"When?" demanded Chiun.

"I don't know," shrugged Remo. "Three . . . four years ago."

"Bird droppings," Chiun hissed. His hand flashed out and slammed the off button on the television set.

He turned to Remo, his hazel eyes filled with anger. "Why did you not tell me?"

"Tell you what?"

"About this Baraka. About King Adras."

"What should I have told you?" asked Remo, puzzlement on his face.

"That King Adras was deposed by Baraka." He looked at Remo in outrage. "Never mind," Chiun said, "I see I shall have to do everything myself. One can not count on a pale piece of pig's ear for anything. Nobody tells me anything. It is all right. I will get along very well by myself."

He turned and walked away from Remo.

"Will you please tell me what the hell this is all about?"

"Silence. Pack your bags. We must leave."

"Mind telling me where we're going?"

"Yes. We are going to Lobynia."

"Why?"

"Because I have work to do. But don't worry. I won't ask you to help. I'll do it myself. I'm used to doing everything myself."

He turned and walked into the other room, leaving behind Remo, who shook his head and said over and over again, "God spare me. God spare me."

Thirty-six hours later, Remo sat facing Dr. Smith in a sealed car in the parking lot of John F. Kennedy International Airport, where cargo shippers no longer counted percentages stolen, but percentages delivered. Remo carried a small Air France bag. He glanced at his watch.

"I didn't order you to come east, Remo," Smith said. "I tried to set up a meeting on the coast."

"I was on my way out of the country."

"This is no time for a vacation, Remo. This oil thing is serious. In a month or so, this country's going to be so short of oil the economy could close down."

Remo looked out the window at the plane.

"Now I just don't know, Remo. We haven't been able to come up with anything. It's just a hunch, but I think Baraka or one of our oil companies was behind those killings."

Remo watched the heat waves from the back of a jet distort the landscape behind the wide airstrip.

"Yes," Smith went on. "I wouldn't be surprised if Oxonoco Oil were behind this. Oxonoco. Have you heard of it?" He waited. "Remo, I'm asking you a question. Did you ever hear of Oxonoco Oil?"

"Do I ever drive a car?"

"Excellent. Now, as I say, I don't know whether it's Baraka or Oxonoco, but I just feel it's one of them."

"One of them what?" asked Remo, who had not been paying attention.

"One of them behind the oil scientists' killings."

"Oh, that," said Remo. "Don't worry about it," said Remo. "I know who's behind them."

Smith looked startled. "You do? Who?"

Remo shook his head. "You wouldn't believe me if I told you." He watched another jet take off and asked, "You done now? I want to catch a plane."

"Damn it, Remo, what are you talking about? You've got a job to do."

Remo looked at Smith and said, "You've got a helluva nerve. Coming here and telling me maybe it's this guy and maybe it's that guy. Maybe these murder attempts are coming from the Martians."

"How do you figure that out?" asked Smith.

"Well, if we don't find new energy sources soon, we'll run out of fuel for rockets and have to stop polluting space. It could be the Martians. I start with the head Mar."

With that Remo was out of the car and headed toward the Air France Terminal. Smith followed him, but in the open area he was forced to speak obliquely. Remo really detected little difference. His mind was miles away, staring at the Rockies.

There he had learned. He worked for Smith and for Smith's organization not because of any moral superiority of one side over another, but because that was what he should do. Just as Chiun had many contracts in his life, Remo could have only one. It was what he had realized looking at the mountain. He was never going to become like the Master of Sinanju, because he was not Chiun. He was Remo and he was the only person who could be what he could be, just as Chiun was Chiun was Chiun. And Smith talked more silliness.

"Remo, this is a maximum priority situation that is crucial."

Remo hopped a curb. Smith puffed after him. A large group of dour-faced people, many in their early twenties and many more in their forties, trudged solemnly into the Air France building. A few girls wore smocks. The men wore rumpled slacks and sports shirts, or else overalls, almost as two sets of uniforms. Some carried signs. "Third World International Youth Conference." He wondered at the large numbers of forty-year-old youths, who seemed to be in the vanguard as the group pushed its way like a small army into the terminal.

"We can't talk here," yelled Smith.

"Good," said Remo, who didn't want to talk anyhow.

"Let's go back to the car and talk."

"Let's not."

They were in the terminal. Chiun was there, seated on a circular cushion, his fourteen lacquered trunks stacked neatly around him. Every so often someone who accidentally or carelessly brushed against one of the large brightly colored trunks would limp away with a little shriek, as if a bee had stung him behind the calf. Chiun sat in delicate innocent repose, his long hands moving so quickly passersby did not see them. The Master of Sinanju did not like strangers lingering near his possessions.

"Chiun, I'm glad you're here," said Smith. "I'm having difficulty reasoning with him." He nodded to Remo, who stood alongside them stolidly, watching the members of the Third World International Youth Conference.

"To reason with the unenlightened is like trying to make buildings by watering stones," said Chiun. He professed the loyalty of the House of Sinanju to Emperor Smith for eternity and a day. But when Smith explained that he wanted Chiun to convince Remo to stay in America for his assignment, Chiun apologized for his failure to understand English very well, but the one thing he could always do was to pronounce "Glory to Smith." Nor did his English improve on the way to the Boeing 747 with Air France blue on its massive white body.

Chiun personally supervised the loading of his trunks, promising great rewards and issuing serious threats in regard to the safety of the fourteen ancient pieces of luggage.

"Don't let him go," Smith yelled to Chiun, who scampered like a fluttering flag around his trunks.

"Glory to Emperor Smith," said Chiun before disappearing through the door toward the boarding ramp.

Smith turned, felt himself rudely pushed aside by the oncoming members of the Third World International Youth Conference, and then found himself facing Remo.

"Remo, you've got to take this oil assignment. It's critical."

Remo focused his eyes on Smith, as if he were seeing

him for the first time. "Smitty, you listen to me. I know who's behind the murders."

"Then why don't you go get him? Why are you going on vacation?"

"First, I'm not going on vacation. Second, I don't have to go get *him*. He will find me. No matter where I go. Good-bye."

Smith rushed back to the terminal desk.

"Where's that plane going?" he asked an Air France clerk.

"Officially and diplomatically to Paris, because it is not allowed to fly directly to Lobynia."

"But that's where it's going, correct?"

The clerk smiled knowingly.

Smith felt relieved. Remo must know something, or else why would he go to Lobynia. The assassins must have been in Baraka's employ. He started to go, feeling satisfied, then he turned. "Could I see the passenger list, please?"

"Certainly, sir." The clerk held forward the list.

Smith had felt good when he had learned the plane's destination. Now as he read the passenger list, he smiled one of his rare smiles. For there, at the bottom of the list, was a name he knew well. Clayton Clogg. The president of Oxonoco Oil.

CHAPTER NINE

"I hope we get skyjacked."

The girl had to shout to be heard over the noise on the plane, and she shouted with an exuberance that was reflected by very erect breasts under a thin white tee shirt.

"Don't you?" she asked Remo.

"Why?" Remo said, still staring past Chiun out the window of the aircraft. Chiun had insisted upon a window seat so that he could watch the engines fall off in time to say his prayers to his ancestors.

"That is the only way I will get my prayers said," Chiun had complained. "If I wait for you to tell me anything, I will never find out anything."

"Damn it," Remo had said, "I didn't know you want to know about Lobynia. How was I supposed to know about some contract the House of Sinanju has had for a thousand years? Do me a favor, will you? Write down who you've got contracts with and I'll hire a clipping service to keep track of them for you."

"It is too late to go making wild promises or excuses," Chiun had said. "I see that I will just have to do everything myself." One of those things was to be sure he had a window seat, and now he sat there, staring resolutely at the wing of the plane which Remo saw appeared to be on securely.

"Why would you like to be skyjacked," Remo repeated, louder this time, so he could be heard over the noise and music and shouting from the front part of the plane.

"It'd be exciting," the girl said. "And besides we'd be doing something. Really doing something. Like we'd be taking part."

"Part in what?"

"The struggle for liberation. The third world. Didn't you ever hear of them? Palestinian refugees. People who want back the land the imperialistic Zionist pigs have taken from them. Accursed Jewish devils. Do you know they took the best land? They have forests and lakes and land that grows things."

"The way I understand it," Remo said, "when the Israelis took it over it was just sand. There's no shortage of sand in the area. Why don't the refugees get their own piece of sand and make something grow on it?"

"Aha, see. You've fallen for that swine Jewish propaganda. Those trees were there. Anyone who says otherwise is a CIA stooge. My name is Jessie Jenkins. What's yours?"

"Remo."

"Remo? Remo what?"

"Remo Goldberg."

"Why are you going to Lobynia?" The girl seemed unconcerned that Remo's name was Goldberg. "Are you going to our Third World International Youth Conference?"

"I don't know," said Remo. "I'll have to check my tour guide. I think on Monday I'm doing the desert from two till four. Tuesday I've got sand inspection all day, and Wednesday I'm going to look at Lobynia's tree. Thursday we've got dunes. I don't know if I've got time for the youth conference. Lobynia is so full of things to see. If you like sand."

"You should really try to go to our rally. It'll be exciting. Young people from all over the world there in Lobynia to strike a blow against imperialism. To raise our collective voices high in the cry for international peace."

"And of course this international peace starts by wiping out Israel?" said Remo.

"That's right," came a man's voice.

Remo turned away from the window for the first time to look toward the voice. First his eyes lit upon the girl. She was black, her hair wildly afroed, her skin as smooth and sleek as anthracite. Her features were delicate and precise. She was a beauty in any color.

Behind her, on the other side of the aisle, was the man who had spoken. He wore bib overalls, a dirty tee shirt, and a Roman collar around his neck, above the tee shirt. He looked, Remo thought, like a white parody of a zombie.

"You say something, monsignor?" Remo asked.

"No, not monsignor. Just a simple parish priest. Father Harrigan. And I have suffered."

"That's terrible," Remo said. "No one should have to suffer."

"I've suffered," the priest said, "at the hands of those reactionary elements in our church and in our society who do the bidding of the bloodsucking, imperialist warmongers."

"Like Israel, right?"

"Right," said Father Harrigan, looking downward with a sad expression which he had obviously developed by resolutely feeling sorry for himself. "Oh, those Zionist swine. I'd like to burn them."

"Somebody tried that," offered Remo.

"Oh?" said Harrigan, as if he had never heard of anyone bold enough to steal one of his own, his very own ideas. "Well, whoever he was, if he had done it right, we wouldn't have had all this trouble."

Remo nodded. "I feel sorry for those two hundred million Arabs being picked on by those three million Jews."

"Damned right," said Father Harrigan. "And this won't be settled until we do it with blood."

He nodded his head for emphasis, his carefully coifed gray curls splashing down over his face. He directed his washed-out blue eyes away from Remo and back toward the front of the plane, where other delegates to the Third World International Youth Conference were disrobing each other in the aisles to the tuneless slapping of one guitar.

Remo turned back to Jessie Jenkins, looked her over and pegged her age in the late twenties.

"You're a little old to be traveling with this gang, aren't you?"

"You're only as old as you feel," she said, "and I feel young. Oh, I wish we would be skyjacked."

"No chance of that," said Remo.

"Why not?"

"Why? If the skyjackers robbed everybody on the plane, they wouldn't get twenty cents. And if they held all of you for ransom, the world would cheer, laugh, and tell them not to hold their breath. Skyjackers would have more sense than to nail this plane. The whole passenger list isn't worth capturing."

The black woman leaned closer to Remo. "There's a man in the back who's worth something."

"Oh?"

"Yes. Clayton Clogg. He's president of Oxonoco."

Oxonoco. Remo had heard of that. Right. From Smith. Smith thought Oxonoco might be involved in the murders of the scientists. Remo was about to turn to look at Clayton Clogg, when Jessie said, "But you didn't tell me why you're really going to Lobynia."

"I want to tell Colonel Baraka about an oil substitute I've discovered," said Remo.

"An oil substitute?" The woman was interested.

"Right. He might want to buy it from me. Because if he doesn't, I'll sell it to the West and all this economic blackmail over oil will stop cold."

"I didn't know there was such a thing as an oil substitute."

"There wasn't until I invented one. Go ask your friend, Clogg. Tell him I've invented an oil substitute and you'll find out how important it is."

"I think I'll do that," she said. She got up from her seat and walked toward the back of the plane, where a broad pork-faced man with a pushed up nose and large nostrils sat in the middle of a three-seat section, obviously uncomfortable at being mixed in with such trash.

Remo thought he would watch Clogg's reaction, then he decided he would prefer to contemplate the left wing of the plane.

Chiun spoke: "I have decided."

"Oh, the wing is staying on. Good."

Chiun turned to him with a withering stare. "What are you talking about?"

"Nothing. Forget I mentioned it."

"I already have. It is the way to handle nonsense. I have decided. I am going to talk to this Baraka and give him a chance to abdicate before I do anything else."

"Why? That's not your usual way."

"Yes, it is. The thinking man's way. Avoid violence whenever possible. If I can convince him to leave this throne and give it back to the honorable King Adras, then he may go in peace." Chiun's benign and loving face made Remo instantly suspicious.

"The truth, Chiun. Does Adras owe you money?"

"Well, not exactly. One of his ancestors defaulted on a payment."

"Then your house doesn't have a contract."

"Yes, we do. The payment may just have been delayed. The contract was never ended. The ancestor was probably going to pay. Most people do pay their bills to the House of Sinanju."

"No wonder," said Remo. Across the aisle, Father Harrigan overheard only the last syllable of Chiun's remark. "Jew," he said aloud. "Infidel Jews. Burn them. Got to burn them."

"Ignore him," Chiun told Remo. "He is not a holy man. Anyway, I will talk to this Baraka first."

"Suppose you can't get to see him?"

"I am not selling brushes," said Chiun haughtily. "I am the Master of Sinanju. He will see me."

"He'd better."

"He will."

Chiun resumed staring at the wing, and Remo turned over his shoulder to see how Jessie Jenkins was getting along with Clayton Clogg.

Jessie Jenkins had slid into the empty seat alongside Clayton Clogg.

Clogg looked at her, distaste flaring his already distended nostrils. "I'm sorry, this seat is reserved," he said.

"For whom?" she said.

"It is for my use," Clogg said stuffily.

"Well, since you're not using it, I'll use it till you need it."

"If you don't vacate my seat, I shall call the stewardess," Clogg said.

"What's the matter, Mr. Big Oil Company man, I'm not good enough to sit in your seat?"

"If you wish to put it that way," Clogg said.

"You know, I think the people aboard this plane would like to know that you're the president of the blood-sucking Oxonoco Company."

The thought frightened Clogg who had thought he was traveling unrecognized. Resigned, he said, "Sit there if you like."

"Thank you. I will. Now tell me why you are going to Lobynia and what the oil business is like."

Clogg ignored the first question and took ten minutes to answer the second, carefully explaining how not only his oil company but all oil companies were really benefactors of the public, servants of the people, and how it would be a better world if people would just understand who their true friends were.

Through the lecture, Jessie Jenkins smiled and sometimes giggled.

"What are you going to do," she finally asked, "now that Lobynia has cut off its oil sales to America, and the other Arab countries are going to follow suit?"

"We have plans for massive oil field exploration and development. We will meet our responsibilities to the energy needs of a vibrant, growing country in a vibrant, growing world."

"That's good," she said. "And it takes you five years to find a well and another three years to make it produce oil. What are we going to do for eight years—burn blubber in our lamps?"

Clogg turned and looked at the girl with sudden respect glimmering in his eyes. The question was more pointed than he had expected from a crazed, sex-fiend black revolutionary who didn't wear a bra.

"We'll do the best we can to make our supplies go around."

"And that means raising prices so that they'll go around to the people with the most money."

Clogg shrugged. "The free marketplace, you know."

Jessie Jenkins giggled again.

"See that man up there?" She pointed toward Remo. "You ought to talk to him."

"Why?"

"His name's Remo Goldberg. He's invented an oil substitute."

"There is no such thing. Oil is irreplaceable."

"Was irreplaceable. He's made it expendable."

"And what is this Mr. Goldberg doing on his way to Lobynia?" Clogg asked.

"He's going to sell the formula to Baraka. And if Baraka won't buy, he'll sell it to the West."

"That's interesting," Clogg said, who began to stare at the back of Remo's head long enough and hard enough as though to prove that he did find it interesting.

Later, Jessie Jenkins left Clogg's seat and went to the front of the plane. Clogg waited until he was sure she was forward before walking down the aisle toward Remo and dropping heavily into the seat next to him.

Remo looked at the man.

"Power to the people," said Clogg.

"What people?"

"What people are you on the side of?"

"All people," said Remo.

"Power to all people. I understand you're a scientist."

"That's right," said Remo. So this was the man that Smith thought might be involved in the murders of the scientists back in the states. Unlikely, Remo thought. Killers didn't have pig noses.

"In oil, I understand."

"Right," said Remo. "I work on energy substitutes."

"Where are you employed?"

"I'm not anymore. I'm a private researcher."

"How is your research coming?"

"Fine. I've got an oil substitute."

"That's fascinating," Clogg said. "You know, I don't know much about oil but it sounds like it would be a great thing to have. What do you make your substitute out of?"

"Garbage."

"I beg your pardon?"

"Garbage," Remo repeated. "Rubbish, offal, litter, detritus. The real thing. What comes out of cans on Tuesdays and Fridays, except in New York, where you're lucky to get a pickup once a year."

"That's not possible," Clogg said. "Is it?"

"Of course it is," said Remo, trying to remember some of the things Smith had told him. "What is oil anyway? Animal and vegetable matter, decomposed under great pressure. And what is garbage? Mostly animal and vegetable matter. I've found a cheap simple way to simulate the pressure of millions of years and convert the garbage to oil."

"That's very interesting, Mr. Goldberg. I've heard of experiments like yours."

"Yes, there've been some. Most of the people doing them are dead now."

"That's too bad," Clogg said.

"Yes, isn't it?" Said Remo.

"Kill all Jews," mumbled Father Harrigan across the aisle, and popped a pill into his mouth.

CHAPTER TEN

"Do you have it?" Baraka asked his minister of transportation.

"Yes, sir. Right here. It was very easy, too. All I did was call the French ministry and they got clearance from Paris, and Paris called the aircraft and the aircraft beamed back its entire passenger list to the embassy. And I made them hand-deliver it to me here, because I am not a servant to stand around waiting while they decide to do something, but instead the personal emissary of the great Colonel Baraka."

"Silence," thundered Baraka. "I am not interested in the brilliant techniques you used to outsmart the entire French government to acquire a list of passengers aboard a plane. Did it ever occur to you to call Air France and tell them to read you the list?"

"But suppose they said no?"

"Will you get out of my sight?" yelled Baraka. "Go. Go."

The minister turned and headed for the door.

"Idiot, leave the list," Baraka snarled.

"Yes, sir. Yes, sir," said the minister, unable to understand how he had angered Baraka.

He returned quickly to Baraka's desk, put the list

down, threw a snappy military salute, and backed toward the door, watching Baraka in case the colonel should decide to shoot him.

Baraka waited until the heavy door had completely closed, then reached his hand under the left front of the desk and pressed a small red button. A heavy bolt built into the door frame slid out slowly, into a groove cut in the door's side. Automatically, a red light went on over the door, signifying to Baraka's Lobynian secretary that the ruler for life was busy and must not, must not, absolutely must not, under pain of death, be disturbed.

Teaching the secretary this was a monument to Baraka's perserverance.

At first, Baraka had had only the do-not-disturb light installed. He pressed the button on the day of its installation so that he would not be disturbed, but three minutes later his secretary came in.

He told her gently that he was not to be disturbed when the red light was on; she responded that she had not seen it.

He told her to look for it from now on, before entering his office.

She barged through the red light twice more that day.

The second time, Baraka suggested that she would spend the rest of her life in a brothel servicing goats if she did not respect the red light.

That she regarded this as an idle threat was apparent the next morning when she barged past the red light and into Baraka's office.

Baraka responded by putting a bullet into the fleshy part of her left calf.

She was back at work in two weeks, her leg heavily bandaged.

Baraka had arrived at his office early that day. He

94

heard the secretary arrive. He turned on the red light, then waited.

Five minutes later, she limped into his office, carrying a pile of papers.

Baraka sighed. A minute later he was on the phone to the palace electrician, ordering the bolt to be installed in the door.

The electrician promised it his personal undivided attention, and only six weeks later, the bolt was installed. It was a new Lobynian record, since the installation of just the red light had taken four months.

Now Baraka heard the bolt slide closed, locking the door. He waited while a side door to his office opened and the small Oriental, Nuihc, entered.

"I have the list," said Baraka politely to the man who still terrified him.

"I know that," said Nuihc, his voice low and unmenacing, matching the appearance of his body in black business suit, white shirt, and striped tie.

"I had the minister of transport obtain it," said Baraka.

"I do not care how you got it." Nuihc sat on a sofa on the far side of the room. "Bring it here, wog," he said. "Fetch."

Baraka rose quickly and almost loped across the office, holding the list in front of him, as if offering it to an outraged god.

Wordlessly, Nuihc snatched it from his hand and looked quickly down the rows of names.

"Ah, yes," he said. He looked up smiling.

"You look for someone?"

"Yes. Two men. And here they are. Mr. Park and Remo Goldberg."

"Goldberg? What is a Goldberg doing coming to Lobynia?"

"Do not worry," said Nuihc. "His name is not really

Goldberg. He will not contaminate the magnificently pure stock of the Lobynian people," he added contemptuously.

He looked again at the list.

"Who are all these other people?" he asked.

"One is Clogg. He is the president of Oxonoco. One of the oil companies. The others are delegates to the Third World International Youth Conference. Accursed fools."

"What will this Clogg want?" Nuihc asked.

"I do not know," said Baraka. "No doubt, he is supposed to be here to talk about the oil embargo. His real reason for being here may be to take advantage of the little boys in our city's brothels."

Nuihc looked disgusted.

"And the young people for the conference?"

"They are nothing," said Baraka. "A thing common to the United States. Rich, overfed, spoiled, and reeking of guilt because someone else has never tasted escargot. They will make noise. They will pass resolutions condemning Israel and the West. The really fortunate ones will be beaten up on our streets and this will guarantee them happiness because it will confirm to them that they are worthless creatures fit only for the world's scorn and abuse."

"Do you let them wander around your country?"

"By the beard, no," said Baraka. "I keep them under lock and key. The soldiers are instructed to be brutal with them. They enjoy it."

"Why?" asked Nuihc.

Baraka shrugged. "Their entire lives are spent trying to demonstrate their worthlessness. Our soldiers assist them. They are grateful. They smile for black eyes. They laugh aloud when cut bloody. I think they are sexually gratified with broken bones."

"You know, Baraka, you are not such a total fool as you sometimes seem."

"Thank you. Is there anything I should do about the two visitors you have been looking for?"

Nuihc answered quickly and firmly. "No. Just leave them alone. You do not have enough soldiers for that. When I decide the time is right, I will deal with them."

"Are they of the legend?"

"Yes. Leave them alone."

"As you will," said Baraka.

"Yes," Nuihc agreed. "Remember it. As *I* will."

When the Air France plane landed, armed guards were waiting at the bottom of the boarding ladder.

"Hey, look, real guns," said one of the delegates to the Third World Youth Conference. "Heavy. Real heavy."

The young man was the first one down the ramp of the plane. He grinned at one of the fourteen soldiers who formed a passageway and stuck his finger into the barrel of the man's rifle.

The soldier next to him stepped forward and slammed the butt of his rifle into the young man's jaw, knocking him back onto the ground. Blood poured from the gash on his chin.

The soldier stepped back into line without a sound or a glance at the fallen youth.

A young Army captain approached the plane between the lines of soldiers. "I am the cultural liaison officer," he declaimed. "You will all follow me. Anyone who does not will be shot."

"Hey, did you see that?" asked a black youth of a pimply-faced girl with straight black hair, standing next to him on the top of the plane steps.

"Yes. Serves him right. He got what he deserved. I'm sure the great nation of Lobynia has reasons for what it does. We should just do what we're told, because we're totally unqualified to understand or question their society."

The young black nodded in agreement. After all, how could one argue with the girl who was, back at their New York City college, the chairman of the Free Speech Committee, the president of the antibrutality association, the vice chairman of the crusade to end fascism, and chairperson of the Stop Secrecy in Government Committee, ad hoc Presidential War Crimes division. That she had picketed the White House and the Capitol on fourteen different occasions, often sticking flowers into soldiers' guns, winning nothing more for that than surly glances, did not strike her as ironical. She had no time for irony. She was in Lobynia to help all Americans to see it as an example of what they too could become, if they really tried.

The groups of youths scampered off the plane and marched between the twin lines of soldiers, hard on the heels of the cultural liaison officer. The young man who had been slugged picked himself up and staggered along after them.

Last off the plane were Father Harrigan, Clogg, Remo, Chiun.

Father Harrigan posed dramatically on the top of the plane steps. He raised his arms skyward.

"Lord, thank you for granting my wish to set foot on free soil before I die. Lord, you hear me? I'm talking to you."

His raised voice prompted the soldiers at the bottom of the steps to raise rifles to shoulders and point them at him.

Remo pushed Chiun back in through the door.

"Wait until Marjoe either gets killed or gets down," he said.

Finally, after another long loud demand upon God for his undivided attention, Father Harrigan went down the steps. Remo stood in the doorway watching him. If Har-

place one after another, came fourteen soldiers carrying steamer trunks on their heads or in their arms.

At the head of the entire improbable caravan was the cultural liaison officer who counted cadence.

"Hup, tup, turrip, fourp. Hup, tup, turrip, fourp."

Father Harrigan, resplendent in his bib overalls, tee shirt, and Roman collar, fell in with the martial spirit of the day.

He called out, "Cadence count," then led the way in singing. "One, two, three, four, / We won't fight no fucking war, / One, two, three, four, / We won't fight no fucking more."

"Company, halt," screamed the cultural liaison officer.

When the group had staggered to a stop, he turned and addressed the Americans.

"Never having had the opportunity to visit the United States of America, I do not know what kind of country it is you come from," he began.

"No fucking good," shouted Father Harrigan.

"Right on," shouted someone else.

The cultural officer raised his hands for silence.

"However," he said, "Lobynia is a civilized country. We do not use profanity in the streets. In fact, one who utters an obscene utterance in a public place will have his tongue cut out with a dull knife. Such," he said proudly, "is Lobynia's concern for decent civilized humanity and the sensibilities of other persons."

"It would be good if that priest's tongue were cut out," Remo said.

"He would grow a new one," said Chiun. "Useless appendages always grow back."

"Therefore, I must ask you not to utter obscenities in public places." The cultural liaison officer looked from face to face. "Of course, you will be allowed to think ob-

lowed Chiun, who set out resolutely after the delegates to the Third World International Youth Conference.

"People are always willing to help, if you approach them correctly," Chiun said. Behind him, the noncommissioned officer with the broken rifle was ordering his men into action.

"Move, worthless scum. Into the terminal. We have an opportunity to render service to that fine old gentleman of the Third World. Move now or feel my wrath."

The men suppressed smiles and began marching in military fashion toward the terminal, six of them on the left foot, while six more were on the right foot, and the other soldier was between steps. Behind them, the NCO looked at the broken stock of his rifle in wonderment. He picked it up and carried it, moving behind his men. Going into the terminal, he dropped both pieces of the weapon into a trash basket. It was no great loss. The gun had never fired properly anyway. And ever since it had come back from the repair shop, he had been afraid to test it. The last man had found that the repair shop had somehow stuffed the barrel with solder, and when the man had pulled the trigger on the firing range the backfiring bullet had scored a bullseye. On his face.

Lobynian Airport Number One—named back in those optimistic days when people thought the Lobynians might have a reason to build a second airport—was a mile outside the capital of Dapoli.

The caravan was going to have to make the trip on foot. Lobynia's bus had been out of order for the past three weeks, having its spark plugs replaced.

The seventy young Americans marched between columns of armed soldiers. Straggling along behind them came Remo and Chiun, and behind them, falling into

rigan had had a straw hat, he would have looked like something central casting had sent over for a remake of the *Wizard of Oz,* Kansas segment.

Finally, Remo and Chiun left the plane, with Clogg behind them.

Still waiting at the bottom were the twin lines of soldiers, seven on a side.

Now another uniformed officer came up toward the steps, his face wreathed in a smile.

"Mr. Clogg," he called out. "One of my happiest duties as Minister of Energy is greeting you on your all-too-rare visits."

"Yes, yes, yes," said Clogg. "Let's go. My nerves are shattered after the noisy trip."

"Most assuredly," the energy minister said. He took Clogg's elbow and they turned from the plane.

"Hey, what about us?" called Remo.

The energy minister turned. "I suggest you join your party," he said, waving in the general direction of the seventy-member group of delegates to the Third World Conference. "The guards may become impatient."

He dismissed Remo and Chiun and walked away with Clogg toward a limousine parked on the apron of the landing strip.

Remo shrugged. "Come on, Little Father. We'd better go."

"And what of my luggage?"

"It'll catch up to us. They must have a system for delivering it."

"Look about you, Remo, at this land, and then tell me that. You know they have no system for doing anything."

"Well, we can't stand here all day and night."

"We won't."

Chiun brushed by Remo and walked lightly down the steps to the first soldier on the right side of the line.

"Who is in charge here?" he demanded.

The soldier remained silent, staring straight ahead.

"Answer me, you oil slick," Chiun ordered.

The soldier next in line stepped forward, as he had with the youth who owned the intrusive finger, and smoothly and efficiently, lowered his rifle from his shoulder, grabbed the top of the barrel with his left hand, and with his right hand propelled the butt forward toward Chiun's face.

The rifle never reached the face. It was intercepted by Chiun's thin, frail-looking hand, and then the wooden butt dropped, thudding dully on the sticky tar, and came to rest. The soldier stared in astonishment at the metal barrel still in his hands.

Chiun stepped in front of him. He reached up a hand and put it on the soldier's left shoulder. The soldier's mouth opened to scream. Chiun moved his fingers and the soldier found that no sound would come.

"I will ask *you* now. But only one time. Who is in charge here?"

He released the pressure. "I am the ranking noncommissioned officer," the man said.

"Good," said Chiun. "Now look into my eyes and pay attention. Your men will get my luggage. They are extremely valuable and ancient trunks and they will treat them with great care. If they drop one, you will suffer. If they scratch one, you will suffer. If they somehow fail to carry out the assignment, you will suffer. But if they do everything correctly, you may live to see another day dawn upon your worthless life. Do you understand me?" Chiun asked, twisting his fingers into the man's shoulder for emphasis.

"I understand, sir. I understand."

"Come, Remo," Chiun called. "This fine gentleman has offered to help us."

Remo hopped down the stairs from the plane and fol-

scenities in the recesses of your private mind," he added gallantly.

"Let's hear it for the wonderful Lobynian people," said Father Harrigan. "Hip, hip, hooray. Hip, hip, hooray."

The other delegates joined in with a rousing cheer.

The cultural officer nodded, satisfied, turned, and with a "forward march" led the visitors, who could neither talk nor walk freely, on into what they were sure would be an even greater manifestation of even greater personal freedoms, unlike those in hated AmeriKKKKKa.

"Sometimes I think there's no hope for our country," said Remo.

"There has never been any hope for your country," Chiun answered. "Not since you abandoned the good King George and decided to try to rule yourselves. The common man. Ptaah."

"But we've got freedom, Chiun. Freedom," said Remo.

"Freedom to be stupid is the worst slavery of all. Fools should be provided protection from themselves. I like Lobynia," said Chiun and pressed his lips firmly together, opening them again only to shout behind him to the laboring soldiers that their lives were forfeit if they so much as got a sweaty handprint on any of his trunks.

So much for freedom, thought Remo.

The capital city of Dapoli did not loom suddenly in front of them. Rather it grew slowly out of the narrow paved road. First a shack, then what looked like an outhouse, then two shacks, then three. A small store. An occasional bicycle sprawled in sand at the side of the road. Then the appearance of cracked sidewalks. More shacks. And finally when they were surrounded by shacks, they were near the heart of the city. Shacks and gas stations, Remo observed.

The cultural liaison officer raised a hand to halt the group. He waved them to the side of the road because traffic now had grown dangerously heavy, sometimes as much as one car a minute passed their group. He mounted the chipped and broken sidewalk to address them.

"We are now going to a funeral of state for brave Lobynian commandoes killed carrying the message of freedom and glory into the heartland of the Zionist pigs. After that, you will be taken to the barracks which will be your home until the conference is over. The barracks has been created especially for you for this visit and in it, you will find everything you need to be comfortable. There is soap and toilet paper. For privacy, walls have been erected around the slit latrines. Sleeping mats will be provided all. Our glorious leader, Colonel Baraka, has ordered us to spare no expense to bring you all the fine touches that you are used to. No one will be permitted to leave the barracks compound, except to travel in a group to the Revolutionary Triumph building where the conferences will be held. This rule must be observed and security must be maintained because of the presence of so many Zionist spies in our midst. Any questions?"

"Yes," piped up Jessie Jenkins. "When do we get a chance to see Dapoli?"

"Well, little black girl, we are walking through it now, are we not? Keep your eyes open and you will see it." He smiled as he answered, then stopped, looking around for approval.

Father Harrigan led the remainder of the group in good humored laughter.

"Now that the questions are finished, we will continue," said the cultural officer. He led the way through the gutter alongside the sidewalk, deep into the city toward two bigger buildings.

Chiun asked Remo, "Where are we staying?"

"I don't know. I didn't make any reservations, we decided to leave so fast."

Chiun asked the noncommissioned officer leading his trunk-bearers, "Is there a hotel in this desert?"

"Yes, sir," the man said quickly. "The Lobynian Arms."

"Go there and secure us two rooms. Carefully place my belongings in the better of the rooms. Tell them we are coming. What is your name?"

"Abu Telib, master," the frightened soldier said.

"If you fail, Abu Telib, I will find you," Chiun said. "I will seek you out."

"I will not fail, master. I will not fail."

"Be gone."

"How come you get the best room?" asked Remo.

"Rank has its privileges."

CHAPTER ELEVEN

The city square of Dapoli was a trapezoid. Along the narrow back edge ran the long low palace building constructed under King Adras. To the right was the Revolutionary Triumph Building constructed under Colonel Baraka. The buildings were identical, except that having been constructed by foreign workmen, King Adras's building was in much better shape, despite being fifty years older.

The other two sides of the square were bordered by streets, on the far sides of which there were shacks, apparently designed by someone who regarded beads and colored glass as a substitute for both form and function.

The square was alive with people, sounds, and odors. The vile barnyard smell of camels mingled with the smells of burning lamb and the sounds of people talking, shouting, bargaining, singing. Over it hung the piping sounds of wooden flutes common to the area.

"All right, move aside. Everybody out of the way." The cultural attache spoke harshly. He shouldered people aside as he led his brigade of Americans through the square toward the balcony of the palace on which the ceremonies were to be held.

When the group reached the foot of the balcony, the officer turned to the Americans.

"Here you will stay. You will not move from this group. You will not talk to Lobynians. You will show proper obeisance to the great leader, Colonel Baraka, and to the customs and sensibilities of our people. There will be penalties for violators."

Chiun and Remo stood in the rear of the group.

"What are we doing here, Chiun?" asked Remo.

"Shhh. We have come to see Colonel Baraka."

"It's very important to you, Chiun, isn't it?"

"Important, yes. 'Very important?' Maybe."

"It is not at all important to me," said Remo. "What is important is Nuihc."

Chiun turned to Remo, anger narrowing his eyes to two almond shaped slits. "I have told you not to mention in my presence the name of the son of my brother. He has disgraced the House of Sinanju with his evils."

"Yes, Chiun, I know. But he is behind all this. The killings of the oil scientists. Probably the oil boycott too, somehow. And that's what my job is, to end the killings and get the oil turned back on."

"Fool. Think you that he cares about oil? He cares about us. This is all to entrap us. You remember the false agents of your bureau of investigation? A fat one and a thin one. That was his greeting. First fat, then thin. Extremes of weight mean nothing to one who knows the secrets of Sinanju. You remember, you dealt with that once before."

"All right," said Remo. "Let's say he is after us. Let's go get him."

"He will come for us," said Chiun stolidly. "I told you that once before. When we want him, he will find us. We need only wait."

"I'd rather it was on our terms," said Remo, thinking of

his previous battles with Chiun's nephew. The only other man in the world who knew the secrets of the Sinanju assassins lusted for the deaths of Remo and Chiun so he could become Master of Sinanju.

"And I would rather eat duck," said Chiun, his eyes still aimed at the balcony. "The time will be of his choosing."

"And the place?" asked Remo.

"The challenge will come, as it did before and as it must again, in a place of the dead animals. Thus it has been written. It can be no other way."

"The last time, the place of the dead animals was a museum. I don't think Lobynia has any museums," said Remo. He sniffed the air. "I don't even think it's got any bathrooms."

"There is a place of dead animals," said Chium with finality. "There you will be expected to meet his challenge again."

"How do you think it'll go?" asked Remo.

"He has the advantage of being Korean and of the House of Sinanju. On the other hand, you have had the benefit of my personal supervision. He is a defective diamond; you are a highly polished piece of gravel."

"That's almost a compliment."

"Then I withdraw it. *Shhhhh.*"

Onto the balcony stepped a handsome Italian-looking man, dressed in immaculate Army tans. The crowd roared its approval. "Baraka. Baraka. Baraka," they screamed. It quickly built to a chant which seemed to shake the entire city.

The colonel raised his arms for silence. He noticed as he looked down that the loudest screamers were the gang of American hoodlums who had arrived for the Third World Conference.

"He does not look so bad," said Chiun thoughtfully. "He will probably listen to me."

"Probably the mountain will come to Mohammed," said Remo.

In the silence ordered by Baraka, a detail of soldiers now came down the steps of the palace, each four bearing a casket, carrying them out onto the balcony and placing them on the platform behind Baraka.

"Another demonstration of the cowardly Jew," yelled Baraka, pointing at the dozen caskets behind him.

The crowd roared.

When it silenced, Baraka said, "We have come to pay tribute to men who gave their lives to keep Lobynia free."

More screaming and yelling followed this.

It went on that way, each sentence interrupted by cheers and applause, as Baraka told how the men had found out plans for a sneak Israeli attack on Lobynia with atomic pistols, and they set out deep into the heartland of Israel, even into Tel Aviv, and foiled the plan and laid much of that city waste before they were finally overwhelmed by the entire Israeli army.

"But now Tel Aviv knows that no place on earth is safe for them. No place out of the reach of Lobynian justice," Baraka said, touching off screams, even while wondering to himself how Nuihc, who was so small and frail, had been able to kill so many commandoes, who—while they might not have been much as fighting men—had the normal numbers of arms and legs each.

As the cheering continued, Baraka searched the faces of the Americans gathered in a soldier-contained group in front of him. There were the usual assortment of pretty girls. He tried to pick out the prettiest one, in order to invite her to a private dinner at the palace some night during their stay. He gave up the job, but narrowed the number down to three. He would invite all three.

The thing in overalls was, no doubt, a minister of some sort. Mohammed, bless his name, would cringe, were he to have such disciples. It was a wonder that Christ's memory had survived, Baraka thought.

He looked away from Father Harrigan in hurried distaste. In the back of the group staring coldly at him were two men of a different cast. One was American, obviously, but he bore the same sort of hard good looks as Baraka himself. His eyes met Baraka's and there was only cold depth in them, no glimmer of warmth or respect. Even more interesting was the man next to him. He was an aged Oriental in a long gold robe. When he met Baraka's eyes, he smiled and raised an index finger, as if to signal Baraka that he would talk to him later. His eyes were hazel, like Nuihc's, and had the same sort of detached deep placidity that Nuihc demonstrated.

Baraka had no doubt that these were the two men whose arrival Nuihc had been awaiting. The days ahead might yet be interesting, Baraka thought.

"And yet," he yelled, "was a word of this brave strike into the Israel heartland carried in the pig press of the Western world?"

He choked off the cheers by answering his own question. "No. Not one word. The capitalist Zionist press of the world was silent about the bravery of our fallen commandoes."

More cheers. Through them, he heard the priest in overalls yell, "What do you expect when the publisher of the *Times* is named Sulzberger?"

That was good, decided Baraka. He would use that the next time he was interviewed for American television.

He let the crowd shout itself down this time and then said, "We will speed our commandoes' souls to Allah, by prayer." Obediently, the crowd all turned eastward, toward what was now Saudi Arabia and the city of Mecca.

Many of the crowd took prayer rugs from under their garments and spread them out before kneeling on them.

"Pray unto Allah for the repose of their souls," commanded Baraka. He dropped to his knees also, his sharp eyes glinting beneath the visor of his military hat, watching the crowd, making sure there were no guns aimed at him.

The Americans shuffled around, then they too dropped to their knees. All but the hard-looking one and the old Oriental. They stood like two slim trees in a forest of kneeling humanity.

Baraka was outraged. But a hiss came from the windows at the back of the balcony. "Let them be," said Nuihc's voice. "Do not touch them."

Baraka decided to overlook the religious affront. He lowered his head in prayer.

Silence crowned the vast arena.

Then the voice of the prostrate Father Harrigan rose above the crowd.

"God of man, let those responsible for these deaths burn alive in ovens, according to thy grace. Let them singe and scorch in hell for their very whiteness. Let the full measure of vengeance be taken in thy good name. For an eye, let there be not an eye, but a hundred eyes. All according to thy goodness and love, let death run free among the Zionist white devils, the usurpers and rapers of the land. We ask it in the name of peace and brotherhood."

"Not bad," Chiun said to Remo as Harrigan's voice died out. "Especially the part about putting white people in ovens. Did I ever tell you that they were white because God took them out of the oven too soon?"

"Only a hundred times," said Remo, looking around the crowd. "All right, you've seen Baraka. Seen enough?"

"Yes, for now," said Chiun.

Seconds later, Baraka rose to his feet and looked over the kneeling crowd, before signaling it to rise. The two men, the American and the Oriental, were gone, vanished as if the earth had swallowed them up.

He wondered if he would see them again, before Nuihc worked his will upon them.

CHAPTER TWELVE

The Lobynian Arms was about what Remo had expected.

It had been a hovel in the days of its glory. Now, maintenance and operation were exclusively in the control of the Lobynians, who had nationalized the hotel as a national treasure, and had proceeded to turn it into an international disgrace.

The paint was chipped and peeling in the two adjoining rooms that the frightened soldier had secured for Remo and Chiun.

The beds, consisting of dirty, spotted mattresses on twisted metal frames, lacked not only sheets but covers. There was water in the showers, but only cold, the hot water knobs having been removed.

One of the windows in the smaller of the two rooms was broken, which Remo thought should have gotten rid of the stale smell in the room, until he noticed that pouring through the broken glass were the even staler smells of the great Lobynian outdoors.

"Nice place," he said to Chiun.

"It will keep the rain from our heads," said Chiun.

"It never rains in Lobynia."

"That explains the smell. The country has never been washed."

Chiun carefully counted the steamer trunks, satisfying himself that there were still fourteen of them. He opened one and began to pooch around in its innards, finally coming out with a bottle of ink, a long straight quill pen, and a sheaf of paper.

"What are you doing?"

"I will send a communiqué to Colonel Baraka," said Chiun.

"I'm going to call Smith."

What the room lacked in beauty, the telephone service equaled in inefficiency, and it took Remo forty-five minutes and four tries to get the buzzing ring to the Chicago dial-a-prayer whose number he had given the hotel operator.

"The earth is the Lord's and the fullness thereof," came a recorded voice, scratchy from being patched halfway around the world.

"Gimme that old time religion," Remo said dutifully into the telephone, and then heard a whirring and clicking as his voice signal triggered a series of switching operations and finally he heard another click and Smith saying, "Hello."

"This is Remo. We're on an open line."

"I know," said Smith. "There isn't a secure line in that entire country. See anything interesting? Clogg or Baraka?"

"Both of them," said Remo.

"You said you knew who was behind this?" asked Smith cautiously.

"That's right," Remo said, "but I can't tell you yet. I'll keep you posted."

"There is a new element by the way," Smith said. He went on to explain that also aboard the plane was a man who had developed an oil substitute and was going to sell it to Baraka.

"Oh," said Remo casually, "what's his name?"

"Goldberg," said Smith. He was annoyed when Remo laughed, and asked, "What's so funny?"

"You. And all your spies," said Remo. Still laughing, he hung up. So Jessie Jenkins was an operative for the United States. That was the only way Smith could have heard of the oil substitute.

Well, it was good to know. He would keep an eye out for her welfare. At least she wasn't one of the nits.

When he went back into the other room, Chiun was closing his bottle of ink.

"It is done," he said, and handed the long sheet of parchment forward to Remo. He watched anxiously as Remo read.

"Colonel Baraka.

"You have until noon Friday to abdicate. If you do not, there is no hope for you. Give my best to your family."

It was signed: "The Master of Sinanju, Room 316, Lobynian Arms."

"Well? What do you think?" asked Chiun.

"It's got a kind of old world charm about it," Remo conceded.

"You do not think it too weak? Should I have been more forceful?"

"No," said Remo, "I think you've got just the right flavor. I don't know anyone who could have done it better."

"Good. I want to give him a chance to repent."

"Do you think it was a good idea to give him your room number?"

"Certainly," said Chiun. "How else can he contact me to capitulate?"

Remo nodded. "That's true enough. How will you deliver this?"

"I will take it to the palace myself."

"I'll deliver it if you want," said Remo. "I'd like to get out."

"That would be helpful. It is time for my consciousness raising," said Chiun.

Remo took the rolled parchment from Chiun, went downstairs through the dirty unlit lobby and out into the bright sunlight of Dapoli. He absorbed the smells and sounds of the city as he walked the four blocks to the city square.

The palace was ringed with guards and Remo walked casually through the square, looking for one who was an officer. He finally found one with three stars on his shoulders, indicating a lieutenant general. He was walking back and forth before the palace building, informally inspecting the troops.

"General," called Remo moving quietly up behind him. The general turned. He was a young man with a long white scar running down his left cheek.

"I have a message for Colonel Baraka. How do I get it to him?"

"Well, you could send it to him by mail."

"He will get it then?"

"No," the general said. "The mail is never delivered in Lobynia."

"Well, actually, I was more interested in seeing he got the message than in providing a dry run for your mail system."

"Then you might leave it at the front door of the palace."

"Will he get it that way?"

"Not unless you accompany it with a flock of sheep.

One cannot present anything to the supreme commander without accompanying it with a ritual gift."

"Where can I get a flock of sheep?" asked Remo.

"You can't. There are no sheep in Dapoli."

"Is there another way to get a message to him?"

"No," said the general, turning from Remo. Remo clapped a hand on the soldier's shoulder.

"Just a minute. You're telling me that there's no way to get a message to Baraka?"

"Colonel Baraka," the officer corrected. "That's just what I'm telling you."

"Do you know what you're talking about?" asked Remo.

"I am Lieutenant General Jaafar Ali Amin, the Minister of Intelligence. I know what I am talking about," the officer said haughtily.

"Suppose I gave the message to you?"

"I would read it, then tear it up and throw away the pieces. This is not America. You have no special privileges here."

"Suppose, just as a hypothetical case, I told you that if you tore up the message, I would remove your intestines and strangle you with them? What would be your reaction to that?"

"My hypothetical reaction would be to call the guard and have you arrested and create an international incident that would embarrass your nation." He smiled. "Hypothetically, of course."

"You know," Remo said, "that scar on your face is really striking."

"Thank you."

"But it lacks symmetry."

"Oh?"

"Yes. It needs to be part of a pair." With that, Remo's left hand flicked out. His fingers barely seemed to graze the officer's face. It was only after Remo had vanished into the crowd that General Ali Amin realized he soon would have a matching pair of scars.

Remo stopped at a juice stand and ordered carrot juice. He could not go back without having delivered the message. Chiun would go berserk. On the other hand, if he stormed Baraka's palace as seemed to be necessary, Smith would go berserk.

As he was wrestling with the problem, he saw a familiar face.

Jessie Jenkins, her afro a black halo around her head, was being marched along with two other girls that Remo had been on the plane, guarded by a group of four Lobynian soldiers.

"Hey, Jessie," Remo called.

She turned around and smiled. The caravan stopped. The soldiers looked impatiently at the approaching American.

"Where are you going?" asked Remo.

"We're being marched from our compound over there"—she pointed behind the Revolutionary Triumph Buiilding—"to dinner with Colonel Baraka. An invitation."

"Invitation?" Remo said. "At the point of a gun?"

"It seems to be the way they do things around here," Jessie said.

"All right, enough talks," said one of the soldiers.

"Hold your camels," Remo said. "The lady's busy."

"That is no concern of mine. Let us be off," the soldier said.

Remo explained carefully to the soldier that haste makes waste, and then hastily proceeded to waste the soldier's right shoulder which convinced him that they could wait a few moments more.

Remo pulled Jessie aside. "You know we're in the same business?" he said.

"I'm a student," she protested weakly.

"I know. So am I. I'm majoring in foreign governments and threats against the United States. Can you deliver this to Baraka for me?"

She looked at the rolled parchment. "I can try," she said. She took the rolled paper and with her back turned to the soldier, slipped it into her white nylon blouse.

"If you need me, call me," Remo said. "Room 315, Lobynian Arms."

She nodded, turned and rejoined the group to continue the march to the palace. Remo watched them go, admiring the posterior of Jessie Jenkins and feeling pleased with himself. Message delivered and no one dead. Excellent. Chiun would be proud of him.

However, Chiun was not proud of him.

"You mean you did not deliver my missive personally to Colonel Baraka?"

"Well . . . I gave it to someone to give to him."

"Ahhh, this someone. You saw this someone give it to Colonel Baraka?"

"Well, no. Not exactly."

"I see. You did not exactly see this someone give the letter to Colonel Baraka. Which means that you did not see the letter given to Colonel Baraka at all."

"You might say that."

"In other words, you have failed again. I send you out on a simple mission, to deliver a letter, and you come back and tell me well, maybe, but not exactly, and you might say that, and on the one hand this and on the other hand that, but all it means is that you have not delivered my letter."

"Have it your own way."

Chiun shook his head. "It is too late for that. If I had it

my own way, the letter would have been delivered to Colonel Baraka. To no one else. Ah well, what can one expect when he must do everything himself? No one tells me anything and no one helps me do anything."

"You're making a lot out of nothing," said Remo. "Baraka'll get the letter. Wait and see. He'll answer it."

CHAPTER THIRTEEN

But Colonel Baraka did not answer the message, neither that night nor the next morning.

This was not because he had not received the message. As a matter of fact, Jessie Jenkins had placed it personally in Baraka's hand as she and the other two girls sat with him at a small dinner table in an opulent room in the palace, a room whose walls were finished in linen and around the bases of which were pillows, mats, and cushions of all sizes, shapes, and colors.

Jessie had not read the missive, but she wished she had when she saw the reaction it drew from Baraka when he carefully removed the red tie and read it.

The blood seemed to drain from his face. He blotted his face hastily with a napkin, stood up, excused himself from the table, and left the room through a side door.

Baraka went through another door that led into a private corridor of the palace. He walked down the corridor, finally stopping outside a heavy walnut door. He knocked softly.

"Enter," came a thin squeaky voice.

Baraka entered the room. Nuihc sat at a desk, reading the topmost of a stack of newspapers and newsmagazines.

He turned to look at Baraka.

"What requires an intrusion?" he asked.

"This," Baraka said, holding forth the rolled parchment. "It just came."

Nuihc took it and read it quickly. A small thin smile flashed briefly across his face.

He rolled it back up and handed it back to Baraka.

"What should I do about it?"

"Nothing," Nuihc said. "Absolutely nothing."

"What is it, this Master of Sinanju?" Baraka asked.

"He is the man of the legend, come to reclaim the throne of Lobynia for King Adras."

"An assassin?"

Nuihc smiled again. "Not as you know assassins. You are used to dealing with men with guns. With bombs. With knives. But this Master of Sinanju is like no man you have ever seen before. He is himself guns and bombs and knives. Your assassins are like breezes. The Master is a typhoon."

"But then should I not move against him? Place him under arrest?"

"How many more commandoes do you have that are expendable?" Nuihc asked. "For I tell you, you could turn loose all the armies of this godforsaken land, and when they were done, they would still not have touched the robe of the Master." He shook his head comfortingly. "There is only one thing that can save you from that typhoon. That is another typhoon. I am he."

Confused, Baraka began to speak. He was cut off by Nuihc.

"Do nothing. The Master will seek to make contact with you again. Soon, I will be ready to move against him. Leave it to me."

Baraka listened. He had no choice. He nodded, moved toward the door, but with his hand on the knob, he turned. "This Master of Sinanju? Do you think I will ever see him?"

"You have seen him," Nuihc said.

"I have? Who?"

"The old man during the funeral ceremony. That was he," Nuihc said.

Baraka almost permitted himself a laugh, then swallowed it. There was no humor in Nuihc's voice. He had not been joking. And if Nuihc regarded that ninety-pound, aged wraith as dangerous, well, then, Baraka would not quarrel with that judgment.

He nodded and returned to his dinner table, but the pleasure had gone from the prospects of the evening's seduction. His mind kept returning to the two men he had seen during the funeral ceremony. The aged Oriental and the young American. They were something special. This he knew.

"Who gave you the letter?" he asked Jessie as he began to bid goodnight to the surprised girls, who had fully expected to have to fight off a horde of lust-crazed Arabs.

"A man I met on the plane."

"Did he have a name, this man?"

"Yes. His name was . . ." she hesitated momentarily, knowing the virulent anti-Semitism of the Lobynians. "His name was Remo . . . Goldberg," she finally blurted.

Baraka ignored the surname, which she thought was very odd. "So his name is Remo. Remo," he repeated.

The names ran through his mind that night as he lay in his bed. Remo and the Master of Sinanju. And as he finallly drifted into sleep, he saw again the valley leading to the Mountains of the Moon, and remembered the prophecy of "the man from the East who comes from the West."

He woke up, sitting upright in his bed, sweat running down his darkly handsome face. He feared now. And he hoped that Nuihc was a great enough typhoon to stand against the aged one.

It was a strange thing to put one's faith in a man about whom he knew nothing.

There was more to faith than that. And he got out of bed and kneeled at its side, facing East, prostrated himself, and began to pray earnestly and fervently to Allah to protect his servant, Muammar Baraka.

CHAPTER FOURTEEN

"See. He did not get my missive," said Chiun, promptly at noon the next day.

"Maybe he got it and decided to ignore it."

Chiun looked at him in astonishment.

"That is absurd. It was a formal communication from the Master of Sinanju. One does not ignore such things."

"Maybe he doesn't know who you are. Maybe he never heard of Sinanju."

"Why do you persist in that foolishness? Did you not learn when we visited the Loni Tribe that everywhere the name of the Master of Sinanju is known and respected? What more proof do you need?"

"You're right, Little Father," said Remo with a sigh. "The whole world knows about Sinanju. You can't pick up a paper without reading about it. Baraka just didn't get the note." Remo had no desire to argue with Chiun. He was more interested in wondering about Nuihc, where he was and when he would make a move, than in getting involved in one of Chiun's old blood feuds.

"I know he did not get the missive," Chiun said agreeably. "But today he will." And as Remo sat and watched, Chiun withdrew the ink and the pen and the parchment and laboriously drafted a new letter to Baraka. When he was done, he looked up and said politely, "I will deliver this."

"Good for you, Chiun."

"If you had a letter to deliver, I would deliver it for you, too."

"I'm sure you would."

"I would make sure it got into Colonel Baraka's hands."

"Absolutely," said Remo.

"Aha, you say 'absolutely,' but you do not believe Chiun. I can tell. Go ahead. Write a letter to Colonel Baraka. Go ahead, write one for me to deliver."

"Chiun, I don't have to. I believe you, for Christ's sake."

"You say that now, but the question will always remain in your head. Would Chiun really have delivered my letter? Go ahead, write a letter. I will wait."

And because there seemed to be nothing else to do, Remo took a piece of paper and wrote out quickly:

"Colonel Baraka.

"I have discovered an inexpensive substitute for oil. If you are interested in talking to me before I talk to the Western powers, you can contact me in Room 315 at the Lobynian Arms, assuming the hotel does not fall down before your message gets here.

"Remo Goldberg."

"There, Chiun," said Remo folding the note neatly. "Deliver that."

"I will. I will put it in no one's hands but Baraka's."

"You can try," said Remo grudgingly.

"Ahhh, no. You try. I do. That is the difference between being the Master of Sinanju and being . . ."

". . . a pale piece of pig's ear," Remo wearily concluded the sentence.

"Correct," said Chiun.

Minutes later, Chiun left the hotel room. Remo walked downstairs with him because the room was driving him stir crazy and he decided that better than sitting in the room would be sitting in one of the lobby's two chairs, because while the lobby was as ugly as the room, it was bigger. The other lobby chair was filled with the ample, suety, sweating bulk of Clayton Clogg. Clogg saw Remo ease into the chair next to him, and he nodded, as slightly as was possible, to acknowledge Remo's existence.

Remo watched Clogg sweat. So that was Smith's idea of the man behind the killings of the American scientists. Of course, Remo knew what Smith didn't—that Nuihc had masterminded the killings. But had he used Clogg as an instrument? Or Baraka?

"When are you going to make an offer for my oil substitute?"

"Why would I be interested," said Clogg, looking up from a week-old *Times,* his porcine nostrils quivering as if they had just been jammed full of bad smell.

"You don't seem to understand, Clogg. In six months, plants can be busy turning out my substitute, probably as much as 10 percent of the total oil needs of the country. In a year, it'll be 50 percent. Give me eighteen months, and we'll have the technology for towns to build oil-making plants of their own. It'll solve the solid waste problem. No more cities buying gas for their fleets of cars from the oil companies. They'll make their own. And Oxonoco will be looking down the barrel of a gun. A gun loaded with garbage. You'll be lucky to keep a fried chicken franchise."

Clogg watched Remo shrewdly. His nostrils flared.

"You are serious, aren't you, Mr. . . . . er, Goldberg?"

"Of course, I'm serious. I've spent the best years of my life working on this project."

"I just don't seem ever to have heard of you in the area of oil research," Clogg said.

"I've been in affiliated fields," said Remo. "The oil discovery was just a happy accident. Actually, I've been dealing in garbage for the last ten years."

"Where have you worked?"

Remo had known the question would be coming. Smoothly, he answered "Universal Wasting," giving the name of a company that he knew CURE manipulated. He saw Clogg make a mental note of it.

"If you had such a thing, Mr. Goldberg, we might well be interested in making you an offer."

"Straight cash or a percentage of sales?" asked Remo.

"I don't think you'd find a percentage of sales very profitable," Clogg said greasily.

"Why's that?"

"Obviously we could not put such a new development into the market before it had been fully tested. It might be years before it could meet our rigorous standards of quality."

"In other words," said Remo, "it would be buried and forgotten. Like the carburetor that can triple a car's gas mileage."

"That carburetor is a myth. There is no such thing."

"How much cash for an oil substitute?" asked Remo.

"The concept is so unique that a price in six figures might not be out of range. Of course, that's probably not so much when you share it with your fellow researchers."

"No way," said Remo. "There are no fellow researchers and the whole thing is filed up here." He tapped his head. "I wouldn't trust anybody else with my secret."

"That is intelligent of you. There are unscrupulous people in this world."

"That there are."

"Universal Wasting, you say."

"That's right."

Then Clogg was silent again. Remo soon tired of looking up his nostrils and retreated back to his room for his afternoon phone call.

He asked Smith to phony up a cover story for one Remo Goldberg, finally admitting that he was one and the same.

"I wish you had told me yesterday," Smith sniffed.

"Why?"

"Because I wasted a lot of time and money trying to track down an oil researcher named Goldberg."

"I can't do anything about the time, but you can take the money out of Chiun's next gold shipment to Sinanju."

"Be sure to tell him it was your idea," said Smith, in what Remo could swear was his first attempt at humor. Ever.

"One other thing," said Remo. "I don't know anything about international politics, but it might be a good idea if King Adras were ready in the wings, waiting to return to his throne."

"Why?" asked Smith excitedly. "Has something happened to Baraka? Is there . . . ?"

"No," Remo interrupted. "But he might get something in the mail that doesn't sit well."

However such concern about Chiun was unnecessary, Chiun himself told Remo that afternoon.

There had been nothing complicated about it, he told Remo. He had simply gone to the front door of the palace, explained who he was, and in no time at all had been ushered in to see Colonel Baraka. Colonel Baraka had been kind and polite and had treated Chiun with the utmost respect and deference.

"Did he promise to abdicate?"

"He asked for time to consider the prospect. Of course, I granted him an extension until the weekend."

"And you had no trouble getting in to see him?"

"None at all. Why should I? And I delivered your worthless letter, too."

And Chiun stuck to this story, even later when, on the radio which passed for entertainment in Lobynia, there were frenzied news accounts of chaos and violence at the presidential palace. Apparently a group of Orientals, as many as one hundred in number, had assaulted the palace in broad daylight, disabling twenty-seven soldiers. They had been foiled in their attempt to kill Colonel Baraka by his undaunted courage in facing down his attackers.

"Hear that?" Remo asked Chiun.

"Yes. I wish I had been there to see it. It sounds very exciting."

"That's all you've got to say?"

"What else is there?"

Remo bowed in the face of inexorable logic and let the subject drop.

It was still in the mind of Colonel Baraka, however. Nothing else had been in his mind since the aged Oriental had demolished the palace guard and torn open Baraka's bolted door as if it had been made of paper.

His hand still shook when he thought of the diminutive old man who presented him with written demands. He counted himself lucky to have escaped with his life. As soon as he was sure the old man had left, he brought both letters to Nuihc's room.

"They've invaded my palace. What can I do?"

"You can stop chattering as a child," Nuihc said. "Forget the notes. The time has almost come for me to deal with these two."

CHAPTER FIFTEEN

The Third World International Youth Conference opened bright-eyed, bushy-tailed, and noisy at 1:00 A.M. the next morning. Three hundred and fifty delegates from all over the world assembled in the Revolutionary Triumph Building to condemn the United States and Israel for murder and savagery, of which they were not guilty, and to praise the Arabs for murder and savagery, of which they *were* guilty, but which were now labeled heroism and daring.

That was at 9:00 A.M.

At 9:30 A.M., there had been a half-dozen fistfights. Oriental youths, mainly from Japan, wanted to criticize only the Israelis, thus, they thought, scoring points with the oil-supplying Arabs. However, the American delegation would have none of it. They demanded that not only Israelis but all whites be condemned for the basic, cardinal, unforgiveable sin of not being something else other than white.

This provoked the black African delegates to a state of rage, since, misunderstanding the resolution on the floor, they thought it was one of praise and demanded to be included, too. Implicit in their demand was the threat that if their fiat was not heeded, they would eat the white delegates, one at a time.

So it went between 9:00 and 9:30, at which time Jessie Jenkins who had been elected chairperson pro tem by an almost universal nonacclaim, recessed for lunch.

This annoyed most of the spectators in the gallery, who were primarily American newsmen. They found that a half hour was not really enough time for them to find the deep hidden social significance laden with meaning for the entire world contained in what, if the participants had had access to lug wrenches and tire irons, more accurately might have been described as a gang fight.

However, two of the spectators in the gallery were not upset by the early lunch.

In their seats in the balcony, overlooking the large meeting chambers in the Revolutionary Triumph Hall, located next to the Palace, Chiun turned to Remo and said, "Do you understand one word of what has transpired here today?"

"Of course," said Remo. "It's simple. The blacks hate the whites. The whites hate themselves. The Orientals hate everybody. Still to be heard from are the white Ainu of Japan."

Chiun nodded solemnly. "I thought that was what had happened. Tell me, why do they call all come this great distance to confide that they do not like each other? Could they not send each other letters?"

"Aha," said Remo. "They could, but they have no guarantee that you would deliver them yourself, and therefore no guarantee that the letters would arrive. It is simpler this way."

Chiun nodded again, this time unconvinced. "If you say so," he said.

"And why didn't Colonel Baraka contact us last night?" asked Remo.

"He is considering my proposal," said Chiun. "We will hear from him."

The two left their seats, having seen enough of brotherhood in action, and went downstairs to return to their hotel room, but in the first floor they were caught up in swirling pockets of small groups of delegates who were engaging in meaningful dialogue with each other by shouting simultaneously at the tops of their voices.

Remo was for pushing through and out into the sunshine, but he was restrained by Chiun's hand on his shoulder. He turned and saw that Chiun seemed to be interested in one of the conversations which pitted two Orientals against two blacks against two whites. Chiun slid between two of the participants to listen.

"America is the cause of the problem," said one of the Orientals.

Chiun nodded in agreement, then turned to a black who said, "Whites can't be trusted."

Chiun thought this a most worthwhile sentiment.

So, too, did the two whites who insisted that there had been nothing on the earth to rival America's villainy since Darius.

Chiun shook his head.

"No," he said, "Darius was very good."

The six arguers looked at the source of the new voice.

Chiun nodded his head up and down for emphasis. "Darius was very good. The world would be very good, if Darius still reigned. It was not my fault that he was deposed by the Greekling."

"That's right," said one of the blacks. "It was Alexanner that done in old Darius."

"But what about the pharaohs?" shouted one of the white boys, a pimply-faced repository of insecurity, inferiority, and acne.

"At least they knew how to deal with the Jews," said one of the Orientals.

Chiun nodded. "They were all right," he said. "Especially Amenhotep. He paid right on time."

Even in this conversation, that comment seemed to make no sense, and the six young men stopped to look at Chiun.

"It is true," Chiun said. "Amenhotep paid right on time. Long live his memory. And Louis the Fourteenth too."

"What are you talking about?" asked one of the Americans. "You sound like a stooge for the corrupt King Adras. Long live Baraka."

"No," Chiun said. "Adras's ancestor was slow in paying. Otherwise, Adras would again have his throne. If he had, he would answer his mail. Long live Adras."

"Phooey," said the pimply American.

This guaranteed the wisdom of Chiun's position to the two blacks, who joined with Chiun in shouting, "Long live King Adras."

The two hundred and fifty other arguing delegates who had remained thought they were missing something when they heard voices raised louder than their own, and they stopped to listen to the words.

Then, lest they be left out of some very important new movement that could bring a new day of peace of the world, they picked up the chant. "Long live King Adras."

"Long live King Adras."

"Long live King Adras."

They vied with each other to shout the loudest, and soon the Triumph Building resounded with their voices and their echoes.

"Long live King Adras."

"Long live King Adras."

Chiun was leading the cheers as if he were an orchestra conductor, waving his hands in front of him.

Remo turned in disgust and bumped into the very bumpable body of Jessie Jenkins.

"Now that you've got us back to endorsing the monarchy, what's next? Feudalism?" she asked.

"You'll be lucky if he stops at that," Remo said. "How did your dinner go with Baraka?"

"Well, for a man with such a reputation as a woman user, he lost."

"Oh?"

Jessie laughed and the motion rippled her breasts under the light purple top she wore.

"It must have been that note I gave him. The one from you."

"Oh, you did deliver it?"

"Sure. I told you I would. Anyway, I gave it to him. He read it and ran out of the room as if his tail was on fire. Then he came back ten minutes later and ushered us out. Before the ice cream."

"That's interesting," said Remo, who found it interesting. If Baraka had taken the letter to show someone, that someone was probably Nuihc. It would mean he was staying right in Baraka's palace. Why? He was probably waiting for the right moment to move against Chiun and Remo.

"Anybody offer to buy your oil secret yet?" Jessie asked a little too conversationally.

"I've had a few nibbles. And speaking of nibbles, what are you doing tonight for dinner?"

"After the day's rioting is over, we get marched back to our barracks. There we are fed as guests of the Lobynian state. Then we go to sleep. No deviations will be permitted," she said, mocking a deep Nazi accent.

"How about skipping it and having dinner with me?"

"Love to. But I can't get out." To his look of surprise, she added, "Really. We're not permitted to leave the camp."

"Maybe Chiun's right in pushing monarchy. People's democracy seems to have everything except democracy for people," he said.

"No gain without pain," suggested Jessie.

"If you could get out, would you have dinner with me?"

"Sure."

"Be at the main gate of your place at 8:30 sharp."

"They've got guards who look like they'd appreciate nothing better than a chance to shoot you."

"Don't tell them my name is Goldberg," said Remo, and turned away to look for Chiun.

Chiun was approaching him now. The walls and ceiling of the building still resounded with cheers for bonnie King Adras.

"I think we have done enough for today," said Chiun.

Remo could only agree.

At the same time in Lobynia, there was another kind of agreement, this between Colonel Baraka and Clayton Clogg.

At Clogg's invitation, the two men had driven forty miles out into the desert to a mammoth oil field, the main depot to which more than two million barrels of oil daily from Lobynia's eight hundred wells was pumped for storage, and then for shipment by tanker to the rest of the world.

Clogg's black limousine had stopped near the depot, and he told his chauffeur to go for a walk, despite the bone-melting one hundred and thirty degree desert temperature.

"Before you ask," Baraka said, "I will not take steps to end the embargo on oil to your country."

"Fine," said Clogg. "I don't want you to." The look of surprise on Baraka's face passed quickly.

"Then what do you want?" he asked, not deferentially, but not rudely either.

"To ask you a question. What are you going to do with your oil?"

"There will be buyers," said Baraka, detesting this pig-nosed American who instantly had put his finger on the weak spot in the "Arabian salami" tactics.

"Yes," Clogg said. "For a while. The Russians of course will buy to try to hurt the West. But eventually they will have stockpiled and will stop buying excesses because their economy will not stand the drain."

"There is Europe," said Baraka.

"Yes. And Europe will buy your oil until the American economy starts running down and then theirs starts running down. Oil is needed for vehicles and manufacturing and Europe must follow there where America goes."

How like Clogg, Baraka thought, to forget the other uses of oil. The human uses. Heating for homes. The generation of electricity. On his mind were only vehicles and manufacturing. He was so American-industrialist he would have been a cartoon, had he not been too ugly to be a cartoon. Baraka looked out at the acre after acre of storage tanks, oil derricks, complicated equipment, almost all of it operated by computers built by the American oil companies, but he said nothing.

"So you will have a surplus of oil," said Clogg, "and your nation cannot live on oil stockpiles."

"Please dispense with the economics lesson. I take it you have a proposal."

"Yes, I have. Continue the American embargo. However, grant Oxonoco the right to drill on one or several of

137

your offshore islands, with a clear contract that any oil we find is ours to use."

"There is no oil in the offshore islands."

Clogg smiled, a narrow twist of his mouth that made him, God forbid, even uglier than God had planned.

"As they say in my country, so what? Constructing an underground pipeline from this center to the offshore island would be a matter of only months. We could drain off your surplus oil and sell it as our own. Lobynia would get a great deal of private income—for you to dispose of as you see fit."

"And your company would control America's economy," Baraka said.

"Of course."

Baraka stared at his oil wells. A month ago, he would have shot Clogg before the man could finish the first sentence. The effrontery of offering Baraka a bribe. But that was a month ago, when he had still believed that this land could be governed, and he could himself live to an old age in honor and glory. But now there was the prophecy against his life. So Nuihc had promised to protect him from the American assassins. But who would protect him from Nuihc? Baraka found that he had neither stomach nor tolerance to be ordered around like a child for as long as he ruled. He had thought the other day of what life might be like in Switzerland. He looked out now and saw a Lobynian workman trying to open a threaded plug with a wrench. It took him six tries before he found the right wrench. In Switzerland, people made watches and clocks. In Lobynia, people made mess and confusion.

"Could it be kept a secret?" Baraka asked.

"Certainly. Part of our agreement would be that only Lobynian personnel could man the new oil installations for Oxonoco. And . . ."

"You need not finish. I know full well that our

Lobynian craftsmen could work in a false oil depot for fifty years without ever suspecting that there was anything odd about oil coming out of a faucet."

Clogg shrugged. He was glad Baraka had said it and not him. Sometimes these camel-herders were sensitive about the shortcomings of their people.

It might work, Baraka decided. And Clogg, of course, was right. Without some such plan to drain off Lobynia's surplus oil, the economy of the country, already on the edge of disaster, would slide over the brink.

He would have to be careful to keep the plan from Nuihc. But it would work. It would work.

"There is a problem, though," said Clogg, intruding on Baraka's thoughts. Baraka turned to the oil man.

"There is an American," Clogg said. "He has discovered a substitute for oil. His name is Remo Goldberg."

"He has contacted me," said Baraka. "He is a fraud."

Clogg shook his head. "No, he is not. I had him checked by our people. His is one of the most brilliant scientific minds in our country. If allowed to proceed, he could hurt not only your country but my company as well."

"I am not permitted to move against him," said Baraka.

"Not permitted?"

Baraka realized his slip and backed off quickly. "I cannot risk confrontation with the United States government by simply removing one of their citizens."

"Still," Clogg urged, "an accident . . ."

"There have been a number of accidents involving American oil researchers lately," said Baraka.

"I thought you might know something about that," said Clogg.

"And I thought you might know something about it." The two men looked at each other, knowing the way men sometimes do, that each spoke the truth. Baraka wondered though who was right and who was wrong about this Remo Goldberg. An oil scientist or an assassin? Perhaps both. One never knew the lengths of perfidy to which the United States would go.

Clogg looked ahead and mused aloud, "Accidents happen to many people."

"Well, of course, I cannot be held responsible for accidents," Baraka said, giving Clogg what he wanted: a license to remove Remo Goldberg.

The two men talked some more, comparing notes on Remo Goldberg. Both realized that the only person who had any contact with him in Lobynia had been Jessie Jenkins, the buxom black American revolutionary. It was agreed that Baraka would allow one of Clogg's men to be admitted to the Third World compound, where he could keep an eye on Jessie. Baraka also gave his agreement to the plan, but said its announcement must wait a few weeks until "some small business" was accomplished.

Clogg nodded, then leaned forward and blew the vehicle's horn. As if from nowhere, the chauffeur reappeared and was back in his seat, driving the car toward Dapoli.

Baraka noticed the chauffeur was a young Lobynian, barely out of his teens, with smooth light skin, long black curly hair and the petulant lips of a woman. He looked at the chauffeur in mild distaste then asked Clogg if he had enjoyed the pleasures of the city.

Clogg smiled but did not answer. He, too, was looking at the chauffeur.

CHAPTER SIXTEEN

Jessie Jenkins wore a white dress as she waited behind the two guards who stood at attention at the only entrance to the fenced-in compound that housed the jerry-built barracks used by the delegates of the Third World International Youth Conference.

The compound was surrounded by eight-foot-high hurricane fencing, topped by another two feet of barbed wire angled to prevent anyone inside from climbing out.

Remo saw Jessie from a distance as he approached the gate. He also saw a young American with red hair leaning against a nearby barracks building, casually smoking and very uncasually watching Jessie.

Remo stopped just short of the two armed guards and called past them to the young black woman.

"Hi. Can you come out and play?"

"My keepers won't let me." She nodded toward the guards.

"Is that right, gentlemen?" Remo asked them.

"No one is permitted to leave without a written pass."

"And who issues these passes?" asked Remo.

"No one," said the guard. The other stifled a smile.

"Thank you for your courtesy," said Remo. "Come on

down here," he called to Jessie, motioning with his head along the fence.

She walked on her side, he on his, until they were a full hundred feet away from the guards. Glancing over his shoulder, Remo noticed that the redheaded American had moved along with them, still lurking back in the shadows of the compound.

The fence with its inward-facing barbed wire was meant to keep prisoners in, but not to keep visitors out.

Remo waited until he and Jessie had strolled into an area that was on the perimeter of a floodlight's reach, then he grabbed the top of the bar atop the hurricane fencing with both hands, ran two steps up the fence, and thrust out with both feet. The thrusting straightened his body; the upward momentum whirled it around as if he were a weight on the end of a string. His body flipped straight up in the air, then came down, still stiff, on Jessie's side of the fence. Just before his swinging body would have hit the barbed wire, he loosened his grip, tucked his upper body in, cleared the barbed wire, and landed noiselessly on his feet, alongside the amazed Jessie.

"How'd you do that?" she said when she finally spoke.

"Clean living."

"Well, now that you're in, what do we do?"

"Go out, of course."

He led Jessie back toward the front gate.

"How'd the conference go?" he asked.

"Don't ask," she said.

"If I promise not to ask, do you promise not to talk about racism, lack of opportunity, the ghetto, genocide, and oppression?"

"Why, Mr. Goldberg, you don't sound like a liberal at all."

"To me it always seems as if liberals love people in

large masses, and this is the price they pay to hate people individually. I guess I'm not a liberal."

"You don't hate people individually?" asked Jessie.

"Sure I do," said Remo. "But I won't pay the price of having to love everybody in a lump. I reserve the right to decide a bastard's a bastard, just because he's a bastard."

"All right," said Jessie. "That makes sense. No ghetto talk. You've got a deal."

By now, they were within ten feet of the two guards.

With his hand, Remo signaled Jessie to wait while he approached the guards.

"Hi, fellas. Remember me?" he said.

Both guards turned and looked at him, first in surprise then in annoyance.

"What are you doing here?" they said.

"I went to get two passes to leave this place."

"Yes," the bigger guard said suspiciously.

"I have them right here."

"Yes?" said the guard again.

Remo reached his hand into his trousers pocket and brought it out slowly, in a fist. He held it up between the two guards.

"Right here," he said.

They leaned forward to look.

"Well?" said one of them.

The two guards were leaning close to each other now, almost head to head, when Remo partially opened his hand, uncoiling the little finger and the index finger. He drove these fingers upward.

Each one hit into the forehead of one of the guards, right at that delicate point where veins merge to form a Y close under the skin.

The iron hard fingers like blunted spikes squashed into the veins, closing them for a moment, and bringing on total if short-lived unconsciousness. The two soldiers dropped to the ground, in what seemed, in the darkness, to be a heap of dirty olive drab clothes.

"Come on, Jessie," said Remo.

He helped the girl over the unconscious forms of the two guards. She looked down at them, seemingly unable to look away.

"Oh, don't worry," said Remo. "They'll be all right. Just out for awhile."

"Are you always so aggressive?" she asked.

"I told you, I reserve the right to decide a bastard's a bastard and deal with him in bastardly fashion. These two qualified."

"I have a notion we're going to have an interesting night."

As they walked away from the compound, Remo glanced back over his shoulder to make sure their redheaded companion was following. He was.

"Yes, an interesting night," Remo agreed.

He did not know it would be made even more interesting by the man following the redhead. He was a slight man, an Oriental, in a black business suit. He rarely smiled. His name was Nuihc and he had vowed to kill not only Remo, but Chiun.

This was the first occasion Jessie had had to sample Lobynian nightlife, which was nonexistent.

"You can't get a drink," Remo said. "Baraka doesn't allow alcohol."

"Well, jazz then. There must be a jazz joint."

"Sorry," said Remo. "Baraka's closed down nightclubs too."

"Can we dance?"

"Men and women aren't allowed to dance together."

"Baraka?" she asked.

He nodded. "Baraka."

"I should have poisoned his stuffed cabbage when I had a chance," she said.

"Excuses, excuses."

Remo and Jessie walked along Revolutionary Avenue and finally found one open place, that looked as if it might have once been called a nightclub. It was now labeled a private club "for Europeans only." Remo became a member of the club by slipping twenty dollars to the doorman. Inside, the place still carried memories of its nightclub days. There was a bar on the right. A large room in the back was full of tables leading up to a bandstand, where a belly dancer sweated to the music of three Lobynians playing unnameable string instruments and an unmentionable horn.

"Ain't exactly Birdland," said Jessie.

"Sufficient unto the day," began Remo. Jessie challenged him to finish the quote, but Remo declined since he could not remember the rest.

Remo insisted to the waitress who came to greet them that they be seated in one of the large booths that bordered the main room. The booths were more like small rooms, big enough to seat eight along padded benches around the U-shaped wall. They were screened off from the rest of the room by beaded ropes which could be pulled back if one wanted to watch the floor show. The ropes were infrequently pulled back, since the booths were favorite meeting places for European men and their young male Lobynian lovers.

Remo insisted on a booth. The waitress insisted that she did not understand English or his request. Remo insisted upon giving her ten dollars whereupon the waitress insisted that such a fine gentleman and his lady be seated in one of the fine booths that bordered the room.

As they moved toward the back, Remo glanced behind

him and glimpsed the redheaded American moving toward the bar.

Jessie was upset that there was no alcohol, but finally she shared Remo's order of carrot juice.

"You order that like you're used to it," she said. "A teetotaller?"

"Only when I'm on duty."

"And what kind of duty is that?" asked Jessie, after the waitress had left and Remo had unfastened the clips on the sides of the beaded ropes allowing them to drop and sealing off their booth from the view of the room.

"The same kind of duty you're on," said Remo. "You know. Uncle Sam. The whole gig."

Remo was glad she chose not to be coy. "Then I guess we've got to protect each other, especially since we're being tailed," she said.

"You saw him?" She went up nineteen notches in Remo's eyes.

"Sure. He's been eating me up with his eyes ever since I started waiting for you at the gate."

"He's at the bar now."

"I know," said Jessie. She stopped talking when the waitress pushed aside the beads and placed glasses in front of them. When the waitress left and the beads stopped tinkling together, Jessie leaned across the corner of the table and said, "What are you here for?"

"Clogg," Remo said. "I'm wondering what he's up to."

"That's easy," she said. "He's got some kind of plan to smuggle Baraka's oil into the United States. Washington told me before I left."

"Why didn't they tell me?" complained Remo.

"Easy," said Jessie, sipping her drink slowly and watching Remo over the top of the glass with shrewd eyes. "Your real assignment's got nothing to do with Clogg so they didn't bother to tell you, just as you haven't bothered yet to tell me what your real assignment is."

"All right," he said finally, "you got me. I'm here to figure out how to get King Adras back on the throne." Remo did not like the situation he was in; the girl was smart, and he was not used to this kind of give and take lying.

"Anything else?" she said.

"Yes. One thing. When are we going to make love?"

"I thought you'd never ask," she said. Jessie moved next to Remo on the padded bench. Her arms went around his head and her lips came up to meet his.

Remo responded to her, silently cursing Chiun for the training that had taken all pleasure out of sex and replaced it with discipline and technique.

Jessie gave a slight moan and then Remo was moving his hand under her thin top, doing things to her upper side under her armpit that she had not felt before.

She moaned again. Remo felt her hands come away from his neck and she began to work up her white skirt.

Then in a confluence of bodies and contortions, Remo and Jessie made love on the bench. Her moans and exhortations were buried alive, under the sound of the heavy-hooved belly dancer thumping around on the thin wooden floor to the music of the wooden whistle and string band.

When they were done, Jessie just moved away from Remo and sat stock still, unable to speak for moments. She seemed unaware that her short skirt was still up around her hips, and in fact she did not even move when the waitress barged through the beaded screen to ask if they wanted refills.

Remo nodded yes. When the waitress left, Jessie came to and pulled down her skirt and straightened her sweater.

"Hey now, holy mackerel, Andy," she said.

"I take it that's a compliment," said Remo.

"No, man," said Jessie, her perfect white teeth shiny and brilliant in the ebony majesty of her happy face. "That's no compliment. That's called homage."

"If you're good, I'll invite you back," said Remo.

"I'll be good. I'll be good."

The waitress interrupted them with their drinks and Remo asked: "There was a redheaded man at the bar. Is he still there?"

"Yes, sir," she said.

Remo pressed a bill into her hand. "Don't mention that I asked." The waitress agreed, with an appreciative look toward Jessie, indicating that there might be a payment for the service more preferable than cash.

Remo squeezed her hand lightly, touching a spot between the thumb and index finger, watching her face brighten.

"Hey, I'm the jealous type," said Jessie after the girl had left. "Easy now."

"Just readying the reserves," said Remo. "In case you get uppity."

"I thought we weren't going to talk ethnic," said Jessie and they both laughed and sipped their drinks until Jessie excused herself to go to the ladies' room.

Remo leaned back on the bench, put his toes on the bench on the far side of the table, and concentrated on watching the new belly-dancer through the small cracks between the strands of beads.

She was an improvement over the first. This, Remo determined, because she seemed to sweat less and she smiled occasionally. The first had danced as if her primary interest were in not putting a heavy foot through one of the thin floorboards. This one danced as if there were something more on her mind than mere survival.

She finished one dance to scattered applause from the half-empty room and began another.

And then another.

And then Remo wondered where Jessie was. He waited a few more minutes, then looked out through the beaded drape into the room. She was not to be seen.

The waitress stood in the back of the large room, keeping a watchful eye on the small tables and Remo motioned to her.

She came forward with a smile. "Check, sir?"

"The lady I was with? Did you see her leave?"

"No, sir?"

"Would you check in the ladies' room and see if she is there? Her name is Miss Jenkins."

"Certainly, sir."

A moment later the girl returned to Remo. "No, sir. She is not in there. The room is quite empty."

"Is there another door out of there?"

"Yes sir, there is a door that leads into a back alley."

Remo grabbed bills from his pocket and pushed them into the girl's hand. "Thanks," he said. As he moved toward the ladies' room, he glanced at the bar. The redhaired man was gone.

Remo went into the ladies' room, past the single stall and the small mirror table and chair, to a push-bar fire door. He opened it and went outside, finding himself in a narrow dark alley, black at one end where it ended against an old building, bright at the other end where it admitted the light from Revolutionary Avenue.

And he saw what he had feared, a crumpled pile that looked black against the splash of light from the street, lying against a wall of the alley.

He ran forward. It was Jessie.

She looked up at him, recognized him, and smiled. The blood from her head wound ran slowly down her face.

He saw the wound was serious.

"Who was it?"

"Redhead. From Clogg. Wanted to know about you."

"It's all right," Remo said. "Don't talk anymore."

"S'okay," said Jessie. "I didn't talk at all." And she smiled at Remo again, and then slowly, almost lazily, her eyes closed and her head drooped off to the side.

She was dead.

Remo stood up and looked down at the body of the girl that had only a few minutes ago been warm and bright and loving, and he took pains to remove from himself any feeling of rage or anger that might be found there. When he was sure there was nothing left except cold determination, he simply walked away from her body and went out onto the street.

In the mercury lights that illuminated the street, red blood looked black, and a black spot on the sidewalk to the right of the alley pointed Remo in the right direction.

He caught up to the redheaded man in two blocks.

The man was strolling casually, unconcerned, back toward the hotel where Clogg and Remo both stayed, probably to report, Remo thought.

Moving silently through the light-bright streets, Remo came up alongside the man. The man wore a dark sports shirt and dark slacks. Remo reached out his right hand, spanning it wide, and caught hold of the man's back, just above his belt buckle, grasping the two heavy vertical ropes of muscles that ran up and down alongside the spinal column.

The man gasped in pain.

"You ain't seen nothin' yet," said Remo coldly.

They were passing a tailoring and dry cleaning shop which was closed for the night. Still holding the man's back, steering him with the painful pressure of five iron-hard fingers, Remo used his left hand to smash open the door.

He pushed it open, then propelled the man into the

darkened store ahead of him. Remo stopped to close the door behind him.

The man was leaning against the counter, facing Remo, his eyes glinting brightly in the reflected light from the street.

"What is this, buddy?" he said in an American accent.

"Do you have a knife? A gun?" asked Remo. "If you do, get them out. It'll make it easier for me."

"What are you talking about? I don't have any weapons."

"Then the sap you used on the girl. Get that," said Remo. His voice was cold and knife-edged, as dark as the store, as empty of feeling as death.

"All right, jewboy, if you insist," the man said. He reached into his back pocket and brought out a lead-loaded, policeman's leather blackjack.

"What'd Clogg want you to do?"

"Pump the girl. Find out who you were. I didn't get a chance. She collapsed too fast." Remo could see the man's teeth shine white as he smiled. "You made it easy. Now I can pump you."

"Do that," said Remo. "Do that."

"I'll go easy on you," said the redheaded man.

He came toward Remo, the lead club raised professionally at shoulder level in his right hand, his left hand bent up in front of his face to ward off any punches.

But no punches came. Instead Remo stood there, and allowed him to swing his blackjack toward Remo's temple.

But the blackjack missed, and then the redheaded man felt it plucked from his fingers, as if he were no stronger than a child.

And then his arm was behind his back and he was being propelled toward the back of the store, and he felt a pain in the back of his neck, and the blackness of the store gave way to a greater blackness of his mind and he felt himself fall into unconsciousness.

He woke up moments later to a strange clinking sound.

His back was on something soft, but his mouth felt funny. What was it, he wondered as he moaned into consciousness. And his mouth felt really strange. It was filled with something.

He felt himself choking. His mouth was filled with his teeth. He looked.

There was Remo Goldberg, standing over him, cracking the weighted lead blackjack down casually, rhythmically, into the redhaired man's face, breaking off his teeth one at a time.

The redhead spat, spraying the air with teeth and blood.

The blackjack came down again. More teeth splintered. The redhead tried to get up, but a finger in his solar plexus locked him in place as if he had been pinned to a board.

"Stop," he cried.

Remo stopped.

"What'd Clogg want?"

"He wanted me to pump the girl. Find out who you were. She didn't say anything."

"Why'd Clogg want to know?"

"He's got an oil deal with Baraka. Your formula might threaten it. He wants to know who else knows about it."

"You have anything to do with those dead oil scientists in the United States?"

"No, no," the man protested, and Remo knew he was telling the truth.

"All right, pal."

"What are you going to do to me?" the man asked, frightened to the edge of panic.

"Kill you," said Remo.

"You can't do that."

"There's an interesting difference there in schools of thought," said Remo. "You say I can't, but I say I can. Who's right? In the morning when they find your body, we'll see I am."

And then he slapped the blackjack down into the redheaded man's mouth, shoving it into his throat, canceling out any chance the man had to scream, but stopping just short of the point where the sap would have cut off the redheaded man's breathing.

Now the redhead recognized where he was and why it was soft. He was lying on an ironing table, the professional kind that dry cleaners used to steam creases into clothes.

Remo smiled at him in the darkness, then lowered the top half of the table down onto him.

The redhead felt the heat begin to sandwich his body.

Remo grabbed a coathanger and twisted it through the handles of the top and bottom parts of the ironing table, fastening it together.

He went to the bottom of the table and turned the heat up to full burn, and then pressed the button activating the steamer.

The redhead heard the hiss first, then felt the hot steam begin to blast out of both halves of the board; through his thin summery clothing he felt burning pain as it hit his body.

"You should be well creased by morning," said Remo.

The redheaded man started to talk, tried to say something but couldn't with the blackjack in his mouth.

His frightened eyes searched for Remo.

"Oh, you want something?" said Remo. "Oh, I see. More starch in the collar. Okay." He took a can of spray starch and sprayed it over the redheaded man's face.

"And listen, we give a one-cent rebate for every hanger you bring back. Don't forget now."

The man tried to cried out, but no sound came, and then there was only the sound of the door closing softly.

The man, terrified now, lay hoping for unconsciousness and praying that he would die quickly. Or be saved.

His wish was to be granted.

There was another sound and the door opened. Pressed down, sandwiched in the ironing board, he tried to turn his head toward the door but he could not see.

And then an oily Oriental voice spoke to him.

"Silence," the voice said.

He heard the sound of the wire coat hanger being released, and then blessed relief as the heated top of the ironing table was lifted. And then the blackjack was removed from his mouth.

And then the Oriental voice was asking him questions, about what he had done and why, and what Clogg and Baraka were up to. He answered them all honestly, and finally the voice said, "That is enough."

The redhaired man started to straighten up, mumbling through his broken mouth, "What is your name? Mr. Clogg will want to reward you."

"My name is Nuihc," came the voice. "But no reward is necessary." And then there was pressure that stopped the red-haired man from getting up, and then he felt the blackjack come down again on his face, hard this time, and then everything went black, all black, and he saw, heard, felt nothing anymore because he was dead.

CHAPTER SEVENTEEN

Clayton Clogg had the entire fourth floor of the Lobynian Arms, but he was nowhere on the floor. However, large portions of his retinue who were there were only too glad to tell Remo where Clogg had gone, if he would only stop.

He stopped long enough for one man to gasp that Clogg had gone with two cars full of Oxonoco "special personnel" to a point on the Lobynian coastline facing one of the small offshore islands. There had been a small Oxonoco camp there, before all the gas supplies had been nationalized.

Remo then stopped with another man long enough for that man to procure a map and to show Remo where the Oxonoco camp was, two driving hours out of Dapoli. The map was easy to read. Out of Dapoli led three roads. One went to the coast to the Oxonoco camp, another went inland to the main oil depot, and the third went deep through the desert to the Mountains of Hercules. Maps in America showed golf courses; this map showed oases. There was only one near the Oxonoco camp.

It was after midnight when Remo left. Clogg had a forty-five minute head start. The desert had not yet surrendered its day-baked heat, and the narrow road seemed to steam as Remo drove along it in the Ford which yet another of Clogg's retinue had graciously offered to lend him—if he would only stop.

Remo had wondered enough whether Clogg or Baraka had been Nuihc's henchman. He would take care of Clogg and Chiun would take care of Baraka. The scientists' killings would end; with Adras back on the throne, the flow of oil to America would resume. And then there would only be Nuihc left. But he was in the future. Clogg was now.

Remo began to feel a slight breeze blowing up and he realized he was nearing the coastline. He turned off his lights and continued to drive in the darkness. Up ahead he saw the bulky shapes of two limousines. He turned off his motor, pressed in the clutch, and let his car roll to a stop behind the limousines.

Remo got out of the car and stopped at each of the two black Cadillacs, reaching in under their dashboards and pulling out handfuls of wire. The cars would be of no use unless Clogg had brought electrical engineers with him as well as oil people. And what the hell were "special personnel" for Oxonoco? he wondered.

Noiselessly, Remo moved toward the breeze and heard the sound of the Mediterranean lapping softly on sand. Ahead he saw shapes. He insinuated himself into the darkness and moved into the group. One moment he was not there, the next moment he was and had always been there.

Clogg was talking, pointing out to the sea.

"How far is the island?"

"Only three hundred yards," came a voice near Remo's right.

"We could put that pipeline in, under water, in not more than a week," Clogg said. "But we have to wait for that greasy mule-skinner to make up his mind. Be ready to move as soon as you hear from me."

"Suppose he says no?" asked a voice across from Remo.

"He won't. Did you ever see one of these animals who could resist cash?" There were chuckles all around. "And if he gets sticky," Clogg added, "well, you men have had some experience in that area. It might just be time for Lobynia to have a new lord high commandant," he said contemptuously.

Clogg turned and looked back toward the road. "I wonder where Red is. He should have been here by now."

The man at Remo's right laughed. "He's got this thing about black twiff. He may be taking his time."

"Killing her with kindness," said another.

Then they all laughed and began to walk back toward the two limousines, Remo melting along with them, first seeming to be in one small group, then in another. When they reached the cars, a man called: "Hey, there's another car there. Whose is that?"

Remo backed off a step from the group. "That's mine," he said coldly.

"And who are you?" The voice was Clogg's.

"A man with a star," Remo said. "You can trust that car belongs to the man who wears a star."

The crowd of men moved closer to Remo. One got too close. He *oomphed* and fell, almost as if for no reason at all. So fast had Remo's hand moved that no one else had seen it.

"I can be very friendly," said Remo.

Clogg recognized the voice. "What is it you want, Mr. Goldberg?"

"Nothing much," said Remo. "Just you."

"Men, start the cars," said Clogg. He backed off toward one of the limousines. The man Remo had put to the ground did not stir, not even when Remo reached in under his light jacket and withdrew his revolver.

Remo moved into his own car.

"Hey, these cars won't start." Remo heard voices. He started his Ford and backed it away thirty feet before stopping it. A light pinkish patch appeared in the eastern sky.

"How will we get back? The sun's coming up."

Remo called out. "Easy. You walk."

Clogg protested. The men protested. One man protested so much that he came up to Remo with a gun in his hand. He hit the ground before the gun did.

Remo still held the gun in his hand. He turned on the Ford's headlights and fired a shot into the air over the men's heads. "All right. Everybody drop their guns."

He watched and counted, as the men, blinded by the high beams, complied. Then with another shot into the air, Remo herded them back along the road to Dapoli, Remo behind them driving in first gear, slowly, but fast enough so the men had to walk briskly to avoid being run down.

The sun lingered before making up its mind to rise, then jumped to its act with passion and soon was beating down. The heat shimmered from the sand, the black macadam road absorbing most of the heat and hurting the feet of the men.

Clogg began to lag behind the young men, and twice Remo bumped him with the car. The second time Clogg stumbled but caught himself and almost trotted to get some distance in front of Remo.

"What is it you want?" he called over his shoulder.

"To see you dead."

"How long are we going to walk?"

"Until you die from the heat."

"We could overpower you, you know."

"Try it," said Remo.

The men marching ahead heard Clogg. They knew that only a few hours exposure to the merciless Lobynian sun could weaken a man to the point of death. Fighting was better than giving up. They turned and split into two groups, all eight of them moving toward the car, circling it now.

Remo ignored them and looked toward the left, searching for something.

"Look, men," he called. "Water." He pointed to the left.

The men turned and saw the trees of the oasis that had been marked on Remo's map. They forgot everything else and began to run through the sand toward the trees.

Remo put the car into second and drove through the soft sand, skirting the men. He turned off the engine and was standing beside the car waiting for them when they arrived.

There was, behind him, a pool of crystal water, shaded from the sun by an overhang of palm trees, surrounded by a ring of bushes.

The men saw the water. They saw Remo, too, but ignored him and plunged through the almost knee-deep sand toward the oasis.

"Hold it, men," yelled out Remo. "We just can't have everybody filling up every which way."

"Why not?" one yelled. "There's plenty of water."

"Yes," said Remo holding the gun in front of him. "But we've got to have even distribution. We're going to take all this water and ship it to England."

"Why?" gasped one of the men, panic and confusion fighting for control of his face.

"Because you never can tell when the water shortage is going to hit England."

"Screw you, I'm getting water," one man said and plunged forward.

He was moving past Remo when he was felled by a hand to the throat. His falling body kicked up light puffs of silvery dust and then he did not move.

"All right, men," called Remo. "Now let's do this right. Everybody get in line."

The men sullenly complied.

"Now you've got to wait your turn," said Remo. "Straighten that line out."

The line formed, Clogg in front, and started to move forward.

"Hold it," called Remo. "We can't have any chaos here. It's got to be orderly. Wait your turn."

"It is my turn. I'm first," protested Clogg.

"Oh, no," said Remo. "There's a bird drinking over there. And there's a monkey waiting. You've got to wait. Stay where you are."

Remo hopped up onto the hot hood of the Ford and waited.

"And don't forget. There's a one-spoon limit. No more."

The men just stared at him.

"That's right," Remo said. "One spoon. We've got to have enough for our regular customers."

The bird on the far side of the oasis flew up into one of the trees.

"Can I go now?" said Clogg.

"Wait a minute," Remo said. "This is an even numbered day. Are you odd or even?"

"Even," gasped Clogg.

"Sorry," said Remo. "I don't believe you. You all look like odd numbers to me."

The men snarled and surged forward.

"That's it," Remo said. "Closing down for the day." He hopped off the car and stood before them with his gun. Even though they were frantic, they declined to challenge his weapon.

"Everybody to the car," he said.

The men looked at him, then trudged toward the open convertible. They piled in and watched Remo, half-fearing, half-hoping, and in a flash of hands, Remo put them all to sleep, still alive.

He slid into the driver's seat, started the engine and drove out away from the oasis, toward the limitless sands that stretched away forever on Remo's map, unbroken by so much as a single tree.

As he drove, Remo found a wrench in the glove compartment and reached down to wedge it between the gas pedal and the firewall. It stuck tightly and the motor began to race. Remo threw in the clutch and let the car coast to a stop, then shifted into first gear, grinding the gears past the racing engine.

He let the clutch out slowly and the car powered forward. He estimated that there was an hour's gas left in the car, even in first gear. The men would be out in two hours at least.

Remo waited until the car was moving nicely, tracking straight across the flat straight sand, then he stood up on the seat and jumped out of the convertible. He watched the car continue forward, picking up speed, carrying its unconscious cargo. They would come to when the car had run out of gas. And they would die in the desert.

Remo watched the car leave, then threw it a salute. So they would die. What did they expect?

"You expect more from an American," he mumbled. "And you get it."

Remo turned back toward Dapoli and started out in a

fast trot to the capital city. It was a good day for a run; he had not been getting enough exercise lately.

He saw one car on the way back to the city, but it was on the far road leading from the Mountains of Hercules and he ignored it. He didn't feel like riding anyway.

CHAPTER EIGHTEEN

Remo and Clogg's party had not been the only people on the desert in the predawn darkness.

Colonel Baraka had awakened in his bed with a vague feeling of fear. He glanced around and saw Nuihc standing next to his bed, looking down at him. The small night-light that burned in the room cut Nuihc's soft yellow face into harsh angles of black, and he looked evil and angry.

"Up, wog," said Nuihc.

Without bothering to protest, Baraka rose and dressed, then followed Nuihc wordlessly out of the palace to the back, where they entered a limousine. Baraka got behind the wheel and Nuihc directed him out into the desert on the most southerly road, leading through miles and miles of desert toward the Mountains of Hercules rising in the background.

Baraka spoke to Nuihc several times, but he got no answer, and finally he stopped trying to make conversation.

They were an hour out of Dapoli when Nuihc finally spoke.

"This will do," he said.

Baraka looked at him, and Nuihc snarled, "Stop the car, wog."

Baraka stopped the limousine in the middle of the road, turned off the key and waited.

"I should have known better than to expect honesty from a swineherd," Nuihc said.

Baraka only looked at him. Nuihc was staring out the windshield at the Mountains of Hercules far in the distance.

"I offered you protection from the death forecast for you in the legend and you repaid me with treachery."

"But . . ."

"Silence, wog. It is right that you know my thoughts. I offered you this protection because I wanted, for my own reasons, to dispose of the men who would come to this land to remove you. It was to entrap them that I eliminated those oil scientists in the United States; it was to bring them here that I instituted the oil embargo. It was to throw them off balance that I had you ignore their messages and their warnings. All this was set up by my plan against the day when I would strike them. It was necessary to that plan to keep them here."

"Why?" asked Baraka, a military man considering a military problem. "You know who they are? Why not just eliminate them?"

"Because, wog, I want them to think. They know I am here. I want them to wonder a bit. When will *he* appear? When will *he* strike? It is not the attack that is the pleasure. It is the attenuation of the suspense before the attack."

"So?" said Baraka.

"So, wog, you and your treachery have conspired to rob me of my pleasure."

"No, Nuihc, no," said Baraka earnestly.

"Do not lie to me." Nuihc still looked straight through the windshield, biting off his words crisply, teeth clenched. "You agreed to a private deal with Clogg, the oil man, to divert Lobynian oil to his company, for eventual use in the United States."

Baraka thought to protest, then stopped. There was no point in branding the truth a lie. Somehow Nuihc knew.

"But what does it matter? The embargo to America remains."

"Fool," Nuihc hissed, and for the first time his eyes sparkled with anger. "If I, secluded in the palace, can learn of this plan, how long do you think it will be before the American government learns of it?"

He turned to look at Baraka. "Do not say 'but,' wog. Even for you, it should be simple. Once the government learns that oil will again flow to their country, they will be satisfied, even if the oil flow is by secret means. They will be careful to do nothing to upset the agreement between you and your perverted friend. They will call back the two men I seek. And all my plans will have gone for naught."

Nuihc squinted at Baraka. "Do you see what you have almost done?" He did not wait for an answer. "Out of the car, wog," he said.

Baraka opened the door of the car, but as he scrambled out he took a pistol from a small concealed pocket next to the driver's seat. He had no doubt that Nuihc planned to kill him. He would get Nuihc as soon as he got out the other door. He turned to look over the roof of the car toward the other door.

The door opened. He waited for Nuihc's head to appear. And then Nuihc was at his side. He had come out through the open driver's door. His hand flashed, invisible in the darkness, and the pistol dropped out of Baraka's hand, thudding softly in the sand.

"Fool," said Nuihc. "Do you think I trust a goatherd?"

"What are you going to do?" asked Baraka.

"Kill you, of course."

"But you can't. The legend says that I need fear only an assassin from the East who comes from the West."

"Fool," said Nuihc, and this time his mouth creased in a thin-lipped smile. "I, too, fulfill that prophecy. The blood of the East flows in my assassin's veins. And I came to you from the West. Remember me to Allah."

And there was one slow lazy movement of one hand, and Baraka dropped, dead without a chance to scream or moan or even feel pain, his heart reduced to mush under the protective shielding of his breastbone which had been shattered to powdered chips by Nuihc's hand.

Nuihc did not even look at the body.

He reentered the car and began the drive back to Dapoli. He must move against Chiun and Remo now. His mind concentrated deeply on how he would do it as he drove, so he paid only scant passing attention to a man he saw in the far distance, running along a parallel roadway toward the town of Dapoli.

When Remo returned to his hotel room, Chiun was already up sitting in his meditation posture, staring at a blank wall.

"I'm home, Chiun," said Remo cheerily.

He was answered by silence.

"It was a terrible night," he said.

Silence.

"Didn't you worry about me?"

Chiun continued to stare straight ahead.

Remo was annoyed. "Didn't you worry that Nuihc might have gotten me."

The mention of the unmentionable name brought Chiun alive.

He wheeled toward Remo. "The challenge will come only in a place of the dead animals," he said. "So it is written; so it must be. You can spend all night gallivanting if you want; it is no concern of mine."

Baraka's body was found before noon and Dapoli soon resounded with the news.

Remo and Chiun were still in their rooms, working on balance exercises, when the news came over the radio which Chiun kept on continuously as a substitute for television—almost as if he were hoping the radio set would sprout a picture tube and somehow jump into the broadcast of "As the Planet Revolves."

In stilted formal English, with dirge music playing in the background, the radio announcer said: "The esteemed leader, Colonel Baraka, is dead."

Remo had been hanging by his heels from the slim molding over the front door, catching balls thrown to him by Chiun. The exercise was difficult, and for a normal athlete would have been impossible. Trying to coordinate one's hand and eyes and brain while hanging upside down would have been too much. For Remo it was an exercise necessary to teach him that the body must be able to work under all conditions, regardless of environment.

The exercise went like this: Chiun would throw a ball. Remo would catch it one-handed and roll it back along the floor toward Chiun, six feet away, while Chiun would have already taken another ball from the pile which would be on its way to Remo.

Left. Right. High. Low. Fast. Slow. Remo caught them all and was beginning to get that prideful feeling that comes from a perfect performance. He knew it was perfect. So good, so perfect, that he was sure it might drag an "adequate" from Chiun. From Chiun this was the highest accolade. Only once had Chiun slipped and told Remo something was "perfect" but he caught himself quickly and added ". . . for a white man."

Chiun's arm was drawn back to throw another hard pink ball when the announcer's voice reported Baraka's death. Chiun heard it and threw the ball violently against Remo, so hard that Remo was unable to move before the ball hit him full in the face.

"Goddamn it," he howled.

But Chiun had turned and walked away and was standing next to the radio, listening, his hands clenching and unclenching.

"The illustrious leader's body was found near the Baraka Memorial Road in the middle of the desert on the way to the Mountains of Hercules. A national period of mourning has been proclaimed by Lieutenant General Jaafar Ali Amin, who has assumed leadership of the government.

"General Ali Amin has blamed the Zionist imperialist American-financed swine for the murder of Colonel Baraka. 'It must have taken a dozen assassins to subdue him,' said the general. 'The signs of a struggle were everywhere. He fought bravely against overwhelming odds. The honor and memory of Colonel Baraka will be avenged.' "

Remo rolled to the floor. He paid no attention to the radio.

"Goddamn it, Chiun, that hurt," he said, rubbing his right cheek.

"Silence," commanded Chiun.

Remo was silent. He listened.

Finally, the announcer said that the station would stop broadcasting for three minutes as a memorial to Colonel Baraka and to give people time to take their prayer rugs and pray toward Mecca.

"All right, Chiun," said Remo good-humoredly. "Baraka's dead. Saves you the work."

"It was *him*," Chiun said. "It was him."

His voice was cold, distant, angry.

"So what?" Remo shrugged.

"So what? So a debt owed by the Master of Sinanju must be paid by the Master of Sinanju. It was *my* contract to return King Adras to the throne. *He* has robbed me of my right to fulfill that contract. In the eyes of my ancestors, it will be as if I failed. I am disgraced."

"Oh, come on, Little Father, it's not so bad as all that."

"It is worse," said Chiun. "Such perfidy. I would never have expected it from one who was born into the House."

The announcer's voice repeated the bulletin. Chiun listened to it all the way through, as if hoping the announcer would say that it had all been a mistake. But it was no mistake. Baraka was dead and this time, Chiun greeted the three-minute pause for Baraka's memory with a smash of his right hand that left the ancient wood-cased old radio a mass of splinters. Miraculously, it continued to squawk.

Remo watched Chiun's face. It seemed to have aged twenty years in a few minutes.

The old man turned and walked slowly across the room. He sat on the floor facing the window. His fingers were touched before him, in prayerful supplication. He was silent, staring at the sky.

Remo knew there would be no way to cheer him up; that there was nothing he could say.

The telephone rang.

Almost thankful for the break, Remo picked up the phone.

It was Smith.

"Remo, what the hell are you doing there?"

"What are you talking about?" Remo said testily.

"We heard that Clogg and a lot of his men are dead. And a government agent. A black girl. And now Baraka. Are you running amok?"

"I didn't do it," said Remo. "Not all of them anyway."

"Well, enough's enough," said Smith. "Forgot about the assignment and trying to get the oil turned back on. The government's going to deal with the new president politically and see what happens. I want you and Chiun to come home. Right away."

Remo looked at Chiun, sitting sadly, looking out the window.

"Did you hear me?" asked Smith. "I said, you two come home right away."

"I heard you," said Remo. "Stuff it. We've got things to do."

He hung up the telephone.

He looked again at Chiun, but the old man was deep in a sadness that Remo could not enter, that no one could enter, because it belonged only to the Master of Sinanju. Chiun was what his history and tradition made him.

Just as Remo was Remo and must do what Remo must do. Right now, that was his job. He had been assigned to get the oil turned back on. He would do his job, and if he could, he would do something for Chiun along the line.

Chiun wanted to be alone now, Remo knew, so he walked quietly out of the room and loped the four blocks to the presidential palace. It looked no different. Just as many guards. Only the Lobynian flag showed a change, because it was now flying at half-staff, and Remo noticed that the grommets were starting to pull loose. The huge city square was beginning to fill with people, probably awaiting a message from the new ruler, Lieutenant General Ali Amin.

Well, Remo would see that the first message from the new ruler was interesting.

Remo walked around the back of the building. Six guards and four broken doors later, he stood in front of the new ruler of Lobynia, Lieutenant General Ali Amin.

The general looked at him and almost involuntarily his

hand went up to his right cheek where a long gash had scabbed over, promising to heal into a beautiful white scar.

"Good," said Remo. "You remember me. Now if you want to keep breathing, this is what you're going to do."

While Remo was explaining to General Ali Amin what he was going to do, a message was left for him at his hotel room.

There was a knock on the door. Chiun in his own room heard the knock and then something else. Something sliding.

Chiun went through the adjoining door and saw a white envelope on the floor inside Remo's door. He picked it up, looked at both sides of it, then opened it.

The bare envelope contained a single small sheet of paper. On it was crabbed handwriting that Chiun recognized immediately. It said: "Pig Remo. I wait for you in the intended place. N."

Chiun held the paper in his hands for many minutes, as if absorbing its feel, as if he could pull from its texture a message other than the one that had been written.

Then he dropped the note to the floor and went back to his own room. Not even Chiun could tell how, but now he knew where the appointed place was. The legends of Sinanju said that the challenge must come in a place of the dead animals and now he knew where that place was.

It did not matter to him that the challenge had been meant for Remo. There was only one way for Chiun to redeem his honor as the Master of Sinanju. It would be to visit punishment upon the man who had robbed Chiun of the duty which was his: the duty of removing Colonel Baraka from the throne of Lobynia.

That much was left to Chiun. Slowly he dressed in a two-piece black karate type suit, and slipped thong sandals onto his feet. Then he opened the door and went downstairs.

Minutes later, a terrified taxicab driver floored the gas pedal of his vehicle and headed out on the central road into the desert, toward the vast Lobynian oil storage fields—the place of the dead animals. There, millions of animals had died to create for future ages the oil on which their foolish countries ran. Today Chiun might die. Would he someday be nothing but oil? Not even so much as a memory?

The cab driver whose meter had been ripped out by Chiun's bare hands smiled nervously at his fare, who sat silently in the front seat staring ahead.

"Radio, sir?" he asked.

There was no answer. Taking silence as acquiescence and needing something to cover the sound of his labored breathing, the driver turned on the radio.

The same announcer's voice came on: "General Ali Amin has just concluded his address to the Lobynian people from the balcony of the palace. He has announced the following major steps.

"First, an end to the Lobynian oil embargo against the United States.

"Second, in an effort to bring all of Lobynia into a cohesive world force and to end factionalism, he has issued an invitation to King Adras to join with him in the formation of a new government, recognizing both the monarchy and the right of free people to govern themselves.

"All hail General Ali Amin. All hail King Adras."

Chiun listened and smiled. Remo had done that for Chiun. Remo was really a good-hearted child.

And Chiun was happy it was he, and not Remo, who was going to the desert to face Nuihc's challenge.

CHAPTER NINETEEN

Chiun stopped the cab two hundred yards from the gigantic oil depot, told the driver he would get his reward in heaven, and stepped out into the burning Lobynian sand.

As he had expected, the depot was deserted. There were no people, no signs of activity. Nuihc had not chanced interference in his challenge to Remo.

Slowly the aged Korean moved through the sand, his feet oblivious to any feeling of heat, toward the storage tanks. There was both sorrow and anger in his heart that his brother's son, born into the House of Sinanju, would attempt to disgrace him by killing Baraka. Death was too good for Nuihc, but death was the one punishment that Chiun was not allowed to administer. Because, for ages past, there had been a dictum that the reigning Master of Sinanju could not take the life of anyone from the village. The rule had been instituted centuries before to prevent the village's benefactor from becoming its tyrant. It still bound Chiun, and worse, Nuihc knew it.

And then, too, there was the fact that Nuihc was less than half Chiun's age, and had had access to the secrets of Sinanju since birth, when he had been anointed and designated as he who would one day become Master. How great were Nuihc's skills?

He still yearned to be the Master of Sinanju. Today, the Master would test him.

Chiun stopped before the gigantic red-and-white-striped oil tank and listened. From many miles away, he heard the hushed breeze buffet the coastline of this country. He heard the light scurrying of small desert animals. He heard the sound of oil moving slowly, heavily through a massive four-foot-wide pipe that snaked its way across the desert and ended here in a small concrete blockhouse, where its precious juice was piped from the building through smaller pipes to the rows of tanks.

But he heard nothing else.

Behind the long row of tanks, there were derricks of producing wells, but they too had been shut down for the day. Chiun moved softly through the sand toward the gigantic steel towers.

He stopped just before reaching the towers and turned around. It was as if he were in an amphitheater. He was bounded on three sides by oil tanks, on the back by the oil towers. No better place to be than in an arena.

Chiun stopped, folded his black-robed arms, and spoke, his voice ringing in the sodden stillness of the Lobynian summer.

"I am the Master, come to face the usurper of my duties. Where is he? Does he hide in the sand like a sick and dying lizard? Show yourself."

And a voice answered, ringing in echo off the oil tanks, "Be gone, old man. My challenge is to the white man to whom you have given the secrets. Be gone."

"You have not dishonored the white man," said Chiun. "You have dishonored me and dishonored the memories of all the Masters who have gone before. Show yourself."

"As you will," responded Nuihc's voice, and then he

appeared atop an oil tank sixty yards across the sand from Chiun. Like Chiun, he wore a two-piece black costume, and now he spread his robed arms against the sun-bleached white sky and called out: "You are a fool, old man, for now you must die."

Nuihc looked across the distance to his uncle, contempt on his face, then jumped from the top of the tank. He seemed to float in slow motion. He landed lightly in the sand at the base of the tank and raised his eyes toward Chiun again.

Slowly he began to walk across the sand toward the aged, frail Chiun.

"You are too old, old man. It is time another took your place," Nuihc said.

Chiun did not speak; he did not move.

Nuihc advanced. "And after you are gone, then I shall deal with the pale piece of pig's ear who is your disciple."

Chiun was still silent.

"The buzzards will pick your meatless bones," said Nuihc still advancing, now only twenty yards from Chiun.

And still Chiun did not speak or move.

And then only ten yards separated them, and Chiun slowly raised a hand above his head.

"Stop!" he called and his voice resounded like thunder in the mock arena and Nuihc stopped in mid-stride, as if frozen.

Across the yards, Chiun fixed his steely hazel eyes upon his nephew.

"You should pray to your ancestors for forgiveness," Chiun said softly. "And especially my brother, the father whom you have disgraced. You go now to meet him in another world."

Nuihc smiled thinly. "Have you forgotten, old man, that you may not kill another from the village? I am protected."

"I knew you would hide, like a woman, behind a shield of tradition," Chiun said. "But I will not be untrue to my duties. I will not kill you." He paused, and then his eyes narrowed even further, until they were only thin penciled slits in his face, which now looked like a primitive mask of hatred and doom. Nuihc seemed relieved, but Chiun said, "No, I will not kill you. But I will leave you here in broken pieces and let the sun finish the task I am not permitted to complete."

And then Chiun took a step forward. And another. And another.

And Nuihc backed up. "You cannot do that," he cried.

"Swine," shouted Chiun. "Dare you to lecture the Master on his powers?" And then he jumped through the air toward Nuihc, who turned and fled, running to escape between two of the tanks out into the broad trackless desert.

But Chiun was in front of him. Nuihc turned again. He felt the whir of air pressure and lowered his head fractionally. A yellow hand flashed by, over the top of his long hair. It hit with a crash against the side of one of the tanks, and thick gooey oil poured through the rupture Chiun's blow had made in the steel.

Nuihc gasped and bolted to the right, again heading for an opening. But there ... again ... Chiun stood before him, a spectre of death and destruction in black.

In desperation, Nuihc left his feet and leaped toward Chiun, his feet cocked beneath his body, ready to lash out and smash into the old man's face or body. Chiun stood unmoving as Nuihc flew toward him. Then Nuihc's right leg flashed out, aimed at Chiun's face, but Chiun merely raised his right hand and to Nuihc it felt as if his foot had slammed into a mountain. He dropped heavily onto the sand, but as fast as he hit he was scurrying away in another direction.

He slipped crossing the growing pool of oil that gushed

from the ruptured tank, turning the sand arena into a sticky quagmire, then saw ahead of him one of the two oil towers and ran frantically toward it. He leaped upward, grabbed a crossbar, spun his body around, and then began to climb up the slim pyramidal steel web.

Chiun walked slowly across the sand toward the tower.

Remo returned to his room, pleased with the day's work, hopeful that getting Adras back onto the throne had helped lift Chiun out of his despondency.

"Hey, Chiun," he called as he entered the hotel room. There was no answer and the only sound in the room came from the radio, as the announcer talked about the impact of the oil embargo in making the West understand the unity of the Arab peoples.

"Chiun?"

Remo looked around the room, then went through the door into his room. There he saw the note on the floor.

He picked it up and read it.

"Pig Remo. I wait for you in the intended place. N."

Chiun had gone instead of Remo. But where was the intended place. He carried the note back into the other room. Chiun should not have gone. It was Remo's challenge to meet. Suppose it was a trap? If Nuihc had hurt Chiun in any way, then he would not sleep another night on the earth, Remo vowed. But where was the intended place?

The squawk of the announcer burst into his thoughts and he went angrily over to turn off the radio.

"... and the shortage of fossil fuels has seriously hurt the West's economy ..." Remo snapped it off. The intended place was a place of dead animals. But where?

And then it came, spurred by the radio broadcast. Fossil fuels. Of course. The place of dead animals was an oil field.

Remo dropped the note and ran downstairs. Moments later he was in a taxicab.

The driver looked at Remo's face, drawn tight with anger and fear for Chiun, then looked at the spot on the dashboard where his meter had been until it was removed by an aged Oriental several hours before.

"Do not tell me, sir. You wish to go to our oil fields, correct?"

"Drive," Remo said.

If he could have climbed higher he would have, but he could not, and so now Nuihc hung from the very top of the oil derrick, looking down in fear at Chiun, who stood eighty-five feet below him, his arms folded across his chest.

"The most timid squirrel always seeks the most high branch," Chiun said.

"Be gone," called Nuihc. "We are members of the House. We have no quarrel."

"I go," said Chiun. "Yet hear this. The white man, Remo, is the true heir of Sinanju. Count yourself lucky that he did not come today to meet your challenge. He would not have treated you so kindly."

Nuihc clung to the top of the derrick. The old man would go; Nuihc need only wait. He would live to fight another day.

He watched Chiun slowly unfold his arms below.

Then Chiun drew back his right hand and smashed it against the complex of valves, pipes, and gears at the base of the derrick.

Nuihc heard before he saw. A hiss and then a deep throated rumble. And then far below him, he saw the first bubble of slick black oil slip from the piping Chiun had ruptured, and then it turned into a frothy plume and it was growing stronger and louder, and it surged suddenly into the air, and then it was on him, and the oil choked him and coated him, and its pressure grew greater and greater as the gusher buffeted him, and then his oil-coated hands could hold no longer and he felt them slip, and then he was being carried away from the derrick, high into the sky atop the black chimney of oil.

Chiun looked up from below and saw Nuihc's body carried high into the sky by the eruption of oil. It seemed to bounce atop the black stream for a few moments, before it was flung out into the air, far off into the sand, and the tons of oil arched softly and began to pour down on Nuihc's body.

Chiun watched a moment, then folded his arms again and walked away from the derrick, across the now oil-filled sand arena toward the thin black road that led back to Dapoli.

Remo saw the frail black-clad figure walking slowly along the road, and ordered the cab driver to stop. The cabdriver recognized his fare from before and groaned, but he quickly braked the aged car.

Remo pushed open the back door.

"Chiun," he called anxiously. "Are you all right?"

Chiun looked up at him blandly. "I sleep well. I am well fed. I exercise daily. Why would I not be all right?" He slid past Remo into the backseat and Remo got in behind him, slamming the door.

"Back to town," he told the driver, then turned to look at Chiun. The old man's eyes were closed and a look of peace was on his face.

"Did you have any trouble?" asked Remo.

"Why should I have had any trouble?" asked Chiun, his eyes still closed.

By the time they reached Dapoli he was snoring.

CELEBRATING 10 YEARS IN PRINT
AND OVER 20 MILLION COPIES SOLD!

☐ 41-216-9 Created, The Destroyer #1	$1.95	
☐ 41-217-7 Death Check #2	$1.95	
☐ 40-879-X Chinese Puzzle #3	$1.75	
☐ 40-880-3 Mafia Fix #4	$1.75	
☐ 40-881-1 Dr. Quake #5	$1.75	
☐ 40-882-X Death Therapy #6	$1.75	
☐ 41-222-3 Union Bust #7	$1.95	
☐ 40-884-6 Summit Chase #8	$1.75	
☐ 41-224-X Murder's Shield #9	$1.95	
☐ 40-284-8 Terror Squad #10	$1.50	
☐ 41-226-6 Kill Or Cure #11	$1.95	
☐ 40-888-9 Slave Safari #12	$1.75	
☐ 41-228-2 Acid Rock #13	$1.95	
☐ 40-890-0 Judgment Day #14	$1.75	
☐ 40-289-9 Murder Ward #15	$1.50	
☐ 40-290-2 Oil Slick #16	$1.50	
☐ 41-232-0 Last War Dance #17	$1.95	
☐ 40-894-3 Funny Money #18	$1.75	
☐ 40-895-1 Holy Terror #19	$1.75	
☐ 41-235-5 Assassins Play-Off #20	$1.95	
☐ 41-236-3 Deadly Seeds #21	$1.95	
☐ 40-898-6 Brain Drain #22	$1.75	

☐ 41-238-X Child's Play #23	$1.95
☐ 41-239-8 King's Curse #24	$1.95
☐ 40-901-X Sweet Dreams #25	$1.75
☐ 40-902-3 In Enemy Hands #26	$1.75
☐ 41-242-8 Last Temple #27	$1.95
☐ 41-243-6 Ship of Death #28	$1.95
☐ 40-905-2 Final Death #29	$1.75
☐ 40-110-8 Mugger Blood #30	$1.50
☐ 40-907-9 Head Men #31	$1.75
☐ 40-908-7 Killer Chromosomes #32	$1.75
☐ 40-909-5 Voodoo Die #33	$1.75
☐ 40-156-6 Chained Reaction #34	$1.50
☐ 41-250-9 Last Call #35	$1.95
☐ 40-912-5 Power Play #36	$1.75
☐ 41-252-5 Bottom Line #37	$1.95
☐ 40-160-4 Bay City Blast #38	$1.50
☐ 41-254-1 Missing Link #39	$1.95
☐ 40-714-9 Dangerous Games #40	$1.75
☐ 40-715-7 Firing Line #41	$1.75
☐ 40-716-5 Timber Line #42	$1.95
☐ 40-717-3 Midnight Man #43	$1.95

Canadian orders must be paid with U.S. Bank check or U.S. Postal money order only.
Buy them at your local bookstore or use this handy coupon.
Clip and mail this page with your order

PINNACLE BOOKS, INC.—Reader Service Dept.
1430 Broadway, New York, NY 10018

Please send me the book(s) I have checked above. I am enclosing $_____ (please add 75¢ to cover postage and handling). Send check or money order only—no cash or C.O.D.'s.

Mr./Mrs./Miss _____

Address _____

City _____ State/Zip _____

Please allow six weeks for delivery. Prices subject to change without notice.

the EXECUTIONER by Don Pendleton

Relax...and enjoy more of America's #1 bestselling action/adventure series!
Over 25 million copies in print!

- ☐ 40-737-8 War Against The Mafia #1 $1.75
- ☐ 40-738-6 Death Squad #2 $1.75
- ☐ 40-739-4 Battle Mask #3 $1.75
- ☐ 41-068-9 Miami Massacre #4 $1.95
- ☐ 41-069-7 Continental Contract #5 $1.95
- ☐ 40-742-4 Assault On Soho #6 $1.75
- ☐ 41-071-9 Nightmare In New York #7 $1.95
- ☐ 40-744-0 Chicago Wipeout #8 $1.75
- ☐ 41-073-5 Vegas Vendetta #9 $1.95
- ☐ 40-746-7 Caribbean Kill #10 $1.75
- ☐ 40-747-5 California Hit #11 $1.75
- ☐ 40-748-3 Boston Blitz #12 $1.75
- ☐ 40-749-1 Washington I.O.U. #13 $1.75
- ☐ 40-750-5 San Diego Siege #14 $1.75
- ☐ 40-751-3 Panic In Philly #15 $1.75
- ☐ 41-080-8 Sicilian Slaughter #16 $1.95
- ☐ 40-753-X Jersey Guns #17 $1.75
- ☐ 40-754-8 Texas Storm #18 $1.75
- ☐ 40-755-6 Detroit Deathwatch #19 $1.75
- ☐ 40-756-4 New Orleans Knockout #20 $1.75
- ☐ 40-757-2 Firebase Seattle #21 $1.75
- ☐ 40-758-0 Hawaiian Hellground #22 $1.75
- ☐ 40-759-9 St. Louis Showdown #23 $1.75
- ☐ 40-760-2 Canadian Crisis #24 $1.75
- ☐ 41-089-1 Colorado Kill-Zone #25 $1.95
- ☐ 40-762-9 Acapulco Rampage #26 $1.75
- ☐ 40-763-7 Dixie Convoy #27 $1.75
- ☐ 40-764-5 Savage Fire #28 $1.75
- ☐ 40-765-3 Command Strike #29 $1.75
- ☐ 41-094-8 Cleveland Pipeline #30 $1.95
- ☐ 40-767-X Arizona Ambush #31 $1.75
- ☐ 41-096-4 Tennessee Smash #32 $1.95
- ☐ 41-097-2 Monday's Mob #33 $1.95
- ☐ 40-770-X Terrible Tuesday #34 $1.75
- ☐ 41-099-9 Wednesday's Wrath #35 $1.95
- ☐ 40-772-6 Thermal Thursday #36 $1.75
- ☐ 41-101-4 Friday's Feast #37 $1.95
- ☐ 40-338-0 Satan's Sabbath #38 $1.75

Canadian orders must be paid with U.S. Bank check or U.S. Postal money order only.

Buy them at your local bookstore or use this handy coupon.

Clip and mail this page with your order

PINNACLE BOOKS, INC. — Reader Service Dept.
271 Madison Ave., New York, NY 10016

Please send me the book(s) I have checked above. I am enclosing $_____ (please add 75¢ to cover postage and handling). Send check or money order only—no cash or C.O.D.'s.

Mr./Mrs./Miss _____

Address _____

City _____ State/Zip _____

Please allow six weeks for delivery. Prices subject to change without notice.

by Lionel Derrick

More bestselling action/adventure from Pinnacle, America's #1 series publisher!

☐ 40-101-9	Target Is H #1	$1.25	☐ 40-067-5 High Disaster #22	$1.50
☐ 40-102-7	Blood on the Strip #2	$1.25	☐ 40-085-3 Divine Death #23	$1.50
☐ 40-422-0	Capitol Hell #3	$1.50	☐ 40-177-9 Cryogenic Nightmare #24	$1.50
☐ 40-423-9	Hijacking Manhattan #4	$1.50	☐ 40-178-7 Floating Death #25	$1.50
☐ 40-424-7	Mardi Gras Massacre #5	$1.50	☐ 40-179-5 Mexican Brown #26	$1.50
☐ 40-493-X	Tokyo Purple #6	$1.50	☐ 40-180-9 Animal Game #27	$1.50
☐ 40-494-8	Baja Bandidos #7	$1.50	☐ 40-268-6 Skyhigh Betrayers #28	$1.50
☐ 40-495-6	Northwest Contract #8	$1.50	☐ 40-269-4 Aryan Onslaught #29	$1.50
☐ 40-425-5	Dodge City Bombers #9	$1.50	☐ 40-270-8 Computer Kill #30	$1.50
☐ 40-957-5	Bloody Boston #12	$1.50	☐ 40-363-1 Oklahoma Firefight #31	$1.50
☐ 40-426-3	Dixie Death Squad #13	$1.50	☐ 40-514-6 Showbiz Wipeout #32	$1.50
☐ 40-427-1	Mankill Sport #14	$1.50	☐ 40-513-8 Satellite Slaughter #33	$1.50
☐ 40-851-X	Quebec Connection #15	$1.50	☐ 40-631-2 Death Ray Terror #34	$1.50
☐ 40-851-X	Deepsea Shootout #16	$1.50	☐ 40-632-0 Black Massacre #35	$1.75
☐ 40-456-5	Demented Empire #17	$1.50	☐ 40-674-6 Candidate's Blood #37	$1.75
☐ 40-428-X	Countdown to Terror #18	$1.50	☐ 40-924-9 Cruise Into Chaos #39	$1.75
☐ 40-258-9	Radiation Hit #20	$1.50	☐ 41-114-6 Assassination Factor #40	$1.75
☐ 40-079-3	Supergun Mission #21	$1.25		

Canadian orders must be paid with U.S. Bank check or U.S. Postal money order only.
Buy them at your local bookstore or use this handy coupon.
Clip and mail this page with your order

PINNACLE BOOKS, INC.—Reader Service Dept.
271 Madison Ave., New York, NY 10016

Please send me the book(s) I have checked above. I am enclosing $_____ (please add 75¢ to cover postage and handling). Send check or money order only—no cash or C.O.D.'s.

Mr./Mrs./Miss _____

Address _____

City _____ State/Zip _____

Please allow six weeks for delivery. Prices subject to change without notice.

DEATH MERCHANT
by Joseph Rosenberger

**More bestselling action/adventure from Pinnacle, America's #1 series publisher.
Over 5 million copies of Death Merchant in print!**

☐ 41-345-9 Death Merchant #1	$1.95	☐ 40-078-0 Budapest Action #23 $1.25
☐ 40-417-4 Operation Overkill #2	$1.50	☐ 40-352-6 Kronos Plot #24 $1.50
☐ 40-458-1 Psychotron Plot #3	$1.50	☐ 40-117-5 Enigma Project #25 $1.25
☐ 40-418-2 Chinese Conspiracy #4	$1.50	☐ 40-118-3 Mexican Hit #26 $1.50
☐ 40-419-0 Satan Strike #5	$1.50	☐ 40-119-1 Surinam Affair #27 $1.50
☐ 40-459-X Albanian Connection #6	$1.50	☐ 40-833-1 Nipponese Nightmare #28 $1.75
☐ 40-420-4 Castro File #7	$1.50	☐ 40-272-4 Fatal Formula #29 $1.50
☐ 40-421-2 Billionaire Mission #8	$1.50	☐ 40-385-2 Shambhala Strike #30 $1.50
☐ 22-594-6 Laser War #9	$1.25	☐ 40-392-5 Operation Thunderbolt #31 $1.50
☐ 40-815-3 Mainline Plot #10	$1.75	☐ 40-475-1 Deadly Manhunt #32 $1.50
☐ 40-816-1 Manhattan Wipeout #11	$1.75	☐ 40-476-X Alaska Conspiracy #33 $1.50
☐ 40-817-X KGB Frame #12	$1.75	☐ 41-378-5 Operation Mind-Murder #34 $1.95
☐ 40-497-2 Mato Grosso Horror #13	$1.50	☐ 40-478-6 Massacre in Rome #35 $1.50
☐ 40-819-6 Vengeance: Golden Hawk #14	$1.75	☐ 41-380-7 Cosmic Reality Kill #36 $1.95
☐ 22-823-6 Iron Swastika Plot #15	$1.25	☐ 40-701-7 Bermuda Triangle Action #37 $1.75
☐ 22-911-9 Nightmare in Algeria #18	$1.25	☐ 41-382-3 The Burning Blue Death #38 $1.95
☐ 40-460-3 Armageddon, USA! #19	$1.50	☐ 41-383-1 The Fourth Reich #39 $1.95
☐ 40-256-2 Hell in Hindu Land #20	$1.50	☐ 41-018-2 Blueprint Invisibility #40 $1.75
☐ 40-826-9 Pole Star Secret #21	$1.75	☐ 41-019-0 The Shamrock Smash #41 $1.75
☐ 40-827-7 Kondrashev Chase #22	$1.75	☐ 41-020-4 High Command Murder #42 $1.95

Canadian orders must be paid with U.S. Bank check or U.S. Postal money order only.
Buy them at your local bookstore or use this handy coupon.
Clip and mail this page with your order

**PINNACLE BOOKS, INC.—Reader Service Dept.
271 Madison Ave., New York, NY 10016**

Please send me the book(s) I have checked above. I am enclosing $_____ (please add 75¢ to cover postage and handling). Send check or money order only—no cash or C.O.D.'s.

Mr./Mrs./Miss _____

Address _____

City _____ State/Zip _____

Please allow six weeks for delivery. Prices subject to change without notice.

More bestselling western adventure from Pinnacle, America's #1 series publisher. Over 6 million copies of EDGE in print!

- ☐ 40-504-9 Loner # 1 $1.50
- ☐ 40-505-7 Ten Grand # 2 $1.50
- ☐ 40-506-5 Apache Death # 3 $1.50
- ☐ 40-484-0 Killer's Breed # 4 $1.50
- ☐ 40-507-3 Blood on Silver # 5 $1.50
- ☐ 40-536-7 Red River # 6 $1.50
- ☐ 40-461-1 California Kill # 7 $1.50
- ☐ 40-580-4 Hell's Seven # 8 $1.50
- ☐ 40-581-2 Bloody Summer # 9 $1.50
- ☐ 40-430-1 Black Vengeance # 10 $1.50
- ☐ 41-289-4 Sioux Uprising # 11 $1.75
- ☐ 41-290-8 Death's Bounty # 12 $1.75
- ☐ 40-462-X Hated # 13 $1.50
- ☐ 40-537-5 Tiger's Gold # 14 $1.50
- ☐ 40-407-7 Paradise Loses # 15 $1.50
- ☐ 40-431-X Final Shot # 16 $1.50
- ☐ 40-584-7 Vengeance Valley # 17 $1.50
- ☐ 40-538-3 Ten Tombstones # 18 $1.50
- ☐ 40-539-1 Ashes and Dust # 19 $1.50
- ☐ 40-541-3 Sullivan's Law # 20 $1.50
- ☐ 40-585-5 Rhapsody in Red # 21 $1.50
- ☐ 40-487-5 Slaughter Road # 22 $1.50
- ☐ 40-485-9 Echoes of War # 23 $1.50
- ☐ 40-486-7 Slaughterday # 24 $1.50
- ☐ 41-303-3 Violence Trail # 25 $1.75
- ☐ 40-579-0 Savage Dawn # 26 $1.50
- ☐ 41-309-2 Death Drive # 27 $1.75
- ☐ 40-204-X Eve of Evil # 28 $1.50
- ☐ 40-502-2 The Living, The Dying, and The Dead # 29 $1.50
- ☐ 41-312-2 Towering Nightmare # 30 $1.75
- ☐ 41-313-0 Guilty Ones # 31 $1.75
- ☐ 41-314-9 Frightened Gun # 32 $1.75
- ☐ 41-315-7 Red Fury # 33 $1.75
- ☐ 40-865-X A Ride in the Sun # 34 $1.75
- ☐ 41-250-9 Death Deal # 35 $1.95
- ☐ 41-106-5 Two of a Kind $1.75

Canadian orders must be paid with U.S. Bank check or U.S. Postal money order only.

Buy them at your local bookstore or use this handy coupon.
Clip and mail this page with your order

PINNACLE BOOKS, INC.—Reader Service Dept.
271 Madison Ave., New York, NY 10016

Please send me the book(s) I have checked above. I am enclosing $_____ (please add 75¢ to cover postage and handling). Send check or money order only—no cash or C.O.D.'s.

Mr./Mrs./Miss _____

Address _____

City _____ State/Zip _____

Please allow six weeks for delivery. Prices subject to change without notice.

by William M. James
Apache

More bestselling action/adventure from Pinnacle, America's #1 series publisher!

- ☐ 40-550-2 First Death #1
- ☐ 40-551-0 Knife in the Night #2
- ☐ 40-552-9 Duel to the Death #3
- ☐ 40-553-7 Death Train #4
- ☐ 40-554-5 Fort Treachery #5
- ☐ 40-555-3 Sonora Slaughter #6
- ☐ 40-556-1 Blood Line #7
- ☐ 40-557-X Blood on the Tracks #8
- ☐ 40-558-8 Naked and the Savage #9
- ☐ 40-559-6 All Blood is Red #10
- ☐ 40-560-X Cruel Trail #11
- ☐ 40-355-0 Fool's Gold #12
- ☐ 40-356-9 Best Man #13
- ☐ 40-357-7 Born to Die #14
- ☐ 40-592-8 Blood Rising #15
- ☐ 40-694-0 Blood Brother #17
- ☐ 40-695-9 Slow Dying #18

All books $1.50 each

Canadian orders must be paid with U.S. Bank check or U.S. Postal money order only.

Buy them at your local bookstore or use this handy coupon.
Clip and mail this page with your order

**PINNACLE BOOKS, INC.—Reader Service Dept.
271 Madison Ave., New York, NY 10016**

Please send me the book(s) I have checked above. I am enclosing $_____ (please add 75¢ to cover postage and handling). Send check or money order only—no cash or C.O.D.'s.

Mr./Mrs./Miss _____

Address _____

City _____ State/Zip _____

Please allow six weeks for delivery. Prices subject to change without notice.

George G. Gilman
ADAM STEELE

More bestselling western adventure from Pinnacle, America's #1 series publisher!

- ☐ 40-544-8 Rebels and Assassins Die Hard #1
- ☐ 40-545-6 Bounty Hunter #2
- ☐ 40-546-4 Hell's Junction #3
- ☐ 40-547-2 Valley of Blood #4
- ☐ 40-548-0 Gun Run #5
- ☐ 40-549-9 Killing Art #6
- ☐ 40-575-8 Crossfire #7
- ☐ 40-576-6 Comanche Carnage #8
- ☐ 40-577-4 Badge in the Dust #9
- ☐ 40-578-2 The Losers #10
- ☐ 40-370-4 Lynch Town #11
- ☐ 40-378-X Death Trail #12
- ☐ 40-523-5 Bloody Border #13
- ☐ 40-524-3 Delta Duel #14
- ☐ 40-525-1 River of Death #15
- ☐ 40-526-X Nightmare at Noon #16
- ☐ 40-528-6 The Hard Way #18
- ☐ 41-106-5 Two of a Kind

All books $1.50 each

Canadian orders must be paid with U.S. Bank check or U.S. Postal money order only.
Buy them at your local bookstore or use this handy coupon.
Clip and mail this page with your order

**PINNACLE BOOKS, INC.—Reader Service Dept.
271 Madison Ave., New York, NY 10016**

Please send me the book(s) I have checked above. I am enclosing $_____ (please add 75¢ to cover postage and handling). Send check or money order only—no cash or C.O.D.'s.

Mr./Mrs./Miss _____

Address _____

City _____ State/Zip _____

Please allow six weeks for delivery. Prices subject to change without notice.